# The COWBOYS From Ireland

BOXSET

# Introduction

The Cowboys From Ireland is the thrilling journey of Rhett and Ryan Kearney, two daring cowboys who venture from the Emerald Isle to the heart of Texas. Determined to leave a mark in the United States, they set their sights on the prestigious US National Rodeo Finale, a competition that promises fame and fortune. But the Kearney brothers are unprepared for the most unpredictable twist of fate — falling in love. These rugged heartthrobs find themselves unexpectedly enchanted by two captivating American best friends, upending all their beliefs about love and life. Immerse yourself in this contemporary western romance, where fierce rodeo excitement meets the depth of true love.

These books were previously sold separately as The Irish Cowboy and The Celtic Cowboy.

# The Irish
# COWBOY

## JESSICA MARIN

## RHETT

THE SUN SITS low on the horizon, painting the sky with vivid hues of orange, pink, and lavender. The colors of the sunset only accentuate the emerald color of the grass that's beneath me as I sit and gaze out over my family's land. Dusk is my favorite part of the day; the part where I get to reflect on how the day went, my gratitude toward any accomplishments made, and what I hope for in my future. I inhale the fresh air, willing it to calm my concern for what tomorrow brings.

Tomorrow is the day I leave for the start of the new Pro Rodeo season in America.

It has always been my dream to be part of the Pro Rodeo Cowboy Association and I've worked my ass off to make sure I can legitimately compete with the best of the best. I started my career in Australia, making a name for myself in their rodeo circuit. I had just applied for my Pro Rodeo card, dreaming of my adventures in the United States, when tragedy struck my family, halting my career and dreams.

I was in the middle of my season when I got the phone call that one of the mares we were raising at our family's stud farm had thrown my father off, shattering both of his legs. I left everything behind and got on the first plane back to Ireland. Recovery was long and tenuous for him, so my siblings and I had to step up and take over the family business. My mother inherited the farm from her family and with my father's business sense, they have made it one of the more reputable stud farms in all of Ireland. Being the eldest of the Kearney children, it was always instilled in me that I would take over one day and continue our legacy. After we got my father home from the hospital, my siblings and I split up the responsibilities. I handled the business operations, my brother controlled ground operations, and my sister was in charge of animal care. We became a well-oiled machine, with business actually thriving under our new system. One year into running the business and the same feelings I had for the farm as a child reared its ugly head.

I absolutely hated it.

Hated being tied down to one place, knowing that the future of my family's livelihood was my responsibility. I wanted to get out of Ireland, to travel the world, and the rodeo gave me that opportunity. I'm the happiest when I'm competing, not when I'm breeding horses for other people.

Those eight-seconds on the back of that horse gives me the chance to chase my dreams.

Guilt eats at me like acid burning a hole through my stomach. The pain of disappointing my family silences me from even telling them. I keep hoping that my feelings are only temporary, that I'm just bitter for putting my career on hold. But then I feel selfish for even feeling the way I do. I'm blessed that my family even has a thriving business for me to take over. Taking care of my family shouldn't be a burden—it should be an honor.

The hurricane of my emotions has put me in a permanent foul mood. I used to be known for being the laid back, calm, and happy Kearney child. Now I'm always tense, distant, and moody. The idea of one day being back in the rodeo was my only ray of hope, so I threw myself into training any chance I could get. As soon as my father received clearance to ease himself back into work, I applied again to enter the Pro Rodeo in America.

Now on the eve of my departure, I question whether I'm making the right decision.

*Should I stay here and takeover the family business or follow my dreams?*

The sound of hooves thundering against the ground brings me back to reality. I look over my shoulder to see my younger brother and his stallion barreling toward me. His cowboy hat sits low on his head, his muscular physique on full display without his shirt. Ryan Kearney knows he's a good-looking, son-of-a-bitch and doesn't hold back his charm where the ladies are concerned. He's proud of the fact that he's known as the playboy cowboy. Despite his promiscuous reputation, Ryan is becoming a respected bull rider. He has spent the majority of his young career in Spain's rodeo circuit and feels he's ready to conquer America with me. This will be the first time we're in the same rodeo circuit together and already the media is buzzing with headlines that the cowboys from Ireland are coming to takeover America.

I turn back around and sigh, wishing my solitude wasn't about to be interrupted. Even though I'm close with my brother, we're worlds apart in our views on how to live our lives. While we're both chasing titles and money, Ryan's also chasing skirts. I can understand his mindset since I used to do the same thing, but as I've gotten older, I have higher expectations for myself when it comes to the woman I plan on spending the rest of my life with. Being alone sucks, but I'm not going to settle down with just anyone. I'm more than willing to wait for that special someone who wants me for me, not because I'm Rhett Kearney, International Bronc Rider.

I'm looking for someone who makes me feel again.

"There you are. I've been looking for you," Ryan says while tying his horse to the same tree where my horse is tied. He sits down next to me and is silent while watching the sunset. Sweat glistens off his body and I'm thankful that he smells more like suntan lotion instead of funky body odor.

"You need to stop riding shirtless on the grounds where patrons can see you," I chide, wishing that I didn't have to constantly repeat myself with him. I hate being a nag to my brother—that's what our mom and sister are for.

"Why? I'm gifting free public services to the men of Kildare by providing happiness to their wives when they get a glimpse of my hot body. They see me and then have something to envision when riding their husbands at night." Ryan slaps my back and laughs at his own joke, while I just shake my head at his cockiness. One day that ego is going to get him in some serious trouble.

"When did you get to be such a cocky bastard?" I raise my eyebrow at him, a smile playing on my lips.

"When I realized the lasses preferred me over you." He shrugs his shoulders, his face serious with the exception of the twinkle in his eye.

"You wish," I grumble, not wanting to hear about his latest escapades. Ryan gossips just as badly as our sister, Shannon, does. Normally, I don't mind listening, but today is not one of those days.

"When did you get to be such a moody bastard? It's like you've had a tampon stuck up in you ever since you came home," Ryan comments, sensing that I'm in no mood to joke around today.

*Rip the Band-Aid off and tell him, Rhett.*

"I don't know if I feel comfortable leaving Dad yet," I answer, which is partly the truth. Our father is just now starting to get around without any help and here both of us are about to leave him. I'm just not ready to reveal the whole truth yet to my brother. I'm not ready to see the look of disappointment in his eyes.

*Or in anyone else's eyes for that matter.*

"You've hired extra help and you know Shannon can run this

place in her sleep."

I nod at Ryan's words as our little sister has stepped up and shown us that while we've been away working on our careers, she has been the one working side-by-side with our parents on the farm for years. Even more impressive is that she still managed to do that and be the first one in the family to graduate from the university. She may only be twenty-two, but she's mature beyond her years. She's proven herself to be able to handle the farm better than Ryan and I could've ever imagined.

*Shannon deserves to inherit the farm, not me.*

I chuckle at my stupidity, shaking my head at myself for not realizing this sooner. I look up to see Ryan staring at me, his eyes narrowed, questions blazing from them.

"I don't know what's going on with you and it's obvious you aren't ready to talk about the real reasons for your shitty attitude, but know this, Rhett Malcom Kearney, this is our time to go dominate the same rodeo circuit—together!" He stands up and faces me, excitement in his expression as he looks down at me. "I know you've seen the headlines online. Let's go invade and conquer!" He pumps his fist in the air and I can't help but chuckle at him, his enthusiasm starting to be infectious.

"What if Dad has another accident?" I softly ask, wondering if Ryan would make the right decision.

"Then we come home," he says nonchalantly, as if it's no big deal to just walk away from potentially one of the biggest times in our career. "We can't worry about the unknown, Rhett. What we know is that we're about to embark on one of the most exciting times in our careers and we're doing it together. It would be nice if you were just a little bit more enthusiastic about it."

I see some of his fire start to diminish and I refuse to be the one to extinguish it.

I rise up to my full height and hold out my hand to him. He looks down at it, his questioning eyes returning back to mine.

"Ryan, it would be my honor as your brother and best friend to go together to the Pro Rodeo."

His smile is blinding as he grabs my hand and pulls me hard into him. We hug tightly, slapping each other on our backs like we always do.

"Then let's go get ready to dominate America!"

We mount our horses and as we start to race back to the stables, I can't help but pray that we stay safe and most importantly, injury free, during our time in the States.

## Chapter 2

### TESSA

SPONSORSHIP CONTRACTS SIGNED? *Check.*

Concession food ordered? *Check.*

Barrelmen hired? *Check.*

Photographer hired? *Check.*

Entertainment secured? *Check.*

I run through my to-do list for today, satisfied at how much I've accomplished within a five-hour time period. With three hours left until quitting time, I can start making my to-do list for tomorrow and maybe, just maybe, even start it early.

*Tessa Mandel, the boss babe!*

I smile at my dorkiness because I'm definitely not the boss of Bear Creek Rodeo, nor would I ever want to be. My title might only be administrative assistant, but I've been given the freedom to do as I please here since the general manager knows my work ethic. I give over one hundred percent even though I hate this place.

That's right, I *hate* this place.

Hate is a strong word…

I *loathe* this place.

I loathe being looked down upon because I'm in a "man's world."

I loathe every single cowboy, contractor, or any man with two legs that thinks that I'm going to want to jump into bed with them as soon as they call me darlin'.

I loathe the smell of manure that creeps its way into my lungs every day.

I loathe seeing the animals get used and abused for entertainment.

Some people love living the small-town life, but I'm not one of those people. My heart belongs to the big city of Dallas and the memories of the happy childhood I once had before they were ripped away from me the night my parents died in a car accident. At twelve years old, I was an orphan and forced to live with my father's stepsister, who was my only living relative. She brought me to this godforsaken town and has taken everything of value that my parents left for me, telling me it is owed to her since she had to spend her own money to "raise" me.

She didn't raise me—I raised myself.

Most of the time she was working to make ends meet and if she wasn't working, she was busy with a new guy walking through our house almost every weekend, hoping he would save her. When she realized that he only wanted a quick roll around with her in bed, she would then drink herself into oblivion.

I wasn't going to be like my aunt.

No man was going to save me.

I'm going to save myself.

By the time I was sixteen, I was going to school during the day and waitressing at one of the local restaurants on nights and weekends. Any spare hours available, I babysat. Any way to make money, I was doing it. When the big event of the rodeo came to town, I worked in the concession stand and that is how I got noticed. But it wasn't the general manager that noticed me—it was his son.

Everyone in Bear Creek knew of Ty George. He was the handsome, up and coming bronc rider and son of Caldwell George, the general manager of Bear Creek Rodeo. Ty George had charisma, good looks, and intelligence. Every woman in a fifty-mile radius wanted him.

And for some reason, he set his sights on me.

He was roaming the halls of the concourse in the arena two days before the rodeo that year. I was outside our concession stand, setting up the chips. A lone bag fell to the floor and when I bent down to pick it up, his cowboy boots were right in front of me. I had heard of Ty, but never looked at him. After all, cowboys and rodeos really didn't interest me. But when my eyes roamed up his body to his face and he smiled his devilish smile at me, I was smitten. I thought he was the hottest man in the whole entire universe. I was seventeen years old and had never had a boyfriend before, much less someone who looked like Ty. I naively drank up all the Kool-Aid that he served me for three months before I gave him my most precious gift of all.

My virginity.

I believed Ty when he told me he loved me.

I believed Ty when he said he wanted to marry me.

I believed Ty when he said he was going to take me away from Bear Creek.

I knew something was wrong as soon as he pulled out of me; he was satisfied with his orgasm and I was left in pain from my first-time experience. He never once asked me if I was okay. Never once consoled me through my tears. Never once apologized. My first-time having sex was awful and left me wondering why it wasn't what I imagined it to be like. Why didn't I feel the passion I felt every time he kissed me? Where was all that heat we had together whenever we fooled around? He immediately got dressed once he was done, kissed my cheek, told me he would call me later, and walked out of my house.

And right out of my life.

The next day he flew to Australia to train to be a part of the

Australian Professional Rodeo Association. He knew he was going to Australia all along but didn't plan on telling me since I was never part of his plans. I tried calling him, but he never picked up and refused to return my calls. He even changed his cell phone number and told people around town that he had to break up with me because I was crazy and stalking him.

I was humiliated.

The only two people who knew the truth were my best friend, Adeline, and Ty's father. I had been part of numerous family dinners at the George residence, so Caldwell George knew who I was. To his credit, he also knew what kind of son he had and immediately sought me out.

"Don't cry over my son—he isn't worth your tears," he told me when I couldn't contain my emotions when seeing him. I was mortified to cry in front of him, but unfortunately, Ty got his good looks from his father.

"I have a proposition for you, Tessa. Even though no one in this town would believe you if you decided to bad mouth my son, I would like to keep this little incident quiet. We have a reputation to keep and I don't want anything or anyone to ruin it. I know that despite you being blinded by my son's bullshit, you're a smart cookie. Therefore, I would like to offer you a job as one of my administrative assistants at the rodeo once you graduate."

I started my new job the Monday after graduation.

I may have been a fool when it pertained to Ty George, but I wasn't a fool to turn down his father's offer. It didn't matter to me that Mr. George was trying to keep me quiet to save his son's precious reputation. Ty did enough damage that no one would believe me anyway. Even if they did, Caldwell George was the big man around town and no one was going to cross him. I needed that extra money and with a broken heart, my drive to get out of Bear Creek was in full speed. My heart hardened a little bit more from my experience with Ty and I judged every single one of those rodeo groupies who were hoping to ride off into the sunset with these cowboys. But I was still a human being with emotions and watching them so desperately throw themselves at these men tugged at my heart. I started journaling my whole relationship with Ty and the emotions that came with it. It was surprisingly therapeutic.

Except instead of writing about my broken, sad ending, I gave myself a new ending.

One with a happily ever after.

I sat and stared at my words, not understanding why I would even fabricate what was supposed to be an autobiography. As I looked up to just stare around my living room, my eyes caught sight of a book lying on the end table next to the couch. It was one of my aunt's silly romance novels that she loved to read. Adeline and her mother loved to read them too.

*Why did they love to read these things so much when it wasn't reality?*

Curiosity got the best of me and I picked up my aunt's book and started to read. Before I knew it, I finished the book in three hours and felt something I hadn't felt in a really long time.

Hope.

I became a ferocious reader, getting my hands on every single romance book I could find, reading books from all the sub-genres within the romance category. By the time I turned twenty, I had read over a thousand books and a new addiction was formed.

Books helped me escape from reality.

Books healed my broken heart.

Books inspired me to be a better person.

Books saved me from going down a dark, negative path of becoming a man-hater.

Books gave me hope that everything is going to be okay.

But what books really gave me was inspiration, because I knew I could write a story just as good as the rest of these published authors could. I got out the journal that I wrote in and edited my history with Ty so that it read like a story, changing our names to create characters, and introducing a new hero who would sweep this girl right off her feet. I then plotted out ten more storylines from people I either personally knew or heard of around town. Every one of my books was going to end in a happily ever after because that is what people deserved to have.

Even my witch-of-an-aunt was going to get her happy ending in fiction.

It was that night that my pen name of T.M. Rose was formed. Rose being my mother's first name.

My job with the rodeo enabled me to save enough money to move into an apartment with Adeline and buy myself a used car. I was completely free of my aunt now that I had my own place and transportation. I felt liberated and independent and it only motivated me more to one day be my own boss and not work for anyone else.

Having a car also enabled me to quit my waitressing job and find a weekend gig in Austin, which was only an hour away. The tips and pay were larger there since it was a bigger city. I decided it was worth the time and money to go to bartending school and two months later, I was hired at one of the many bars that lined 6th Street in Austin. The bar was so busy on the weekends that I made back my tuition money from bartending school within that first month. With my weekends now busy in Austin, my nights during the week were the only available time I had to write.

I poured every ounce of energy I could muster into my first book and on the eve of my 22nd birthday, Adeline and I celebrated hitting the publish button on my first novel. I went to bed that night buzzed from alcohol and the anticipation of seeing how large my sales were going to be when I woke up in the morning.

I woke up to *zero* sales.

After getting over the shock and disappointment of what I felt was a failure, I realized that I had outrageous expectations for myself. *How can I sell books when I don't have an audience?* Yes, I researched how to self-publish my own book, but what I didn't take the time to learn was how to market and advertise myself and my book.

Now three years later, I'm proud to say that tonight is the night I will be publishing my tenth book. I really needed those three years to learn the business, make some mistakes, find my presence amongst the book community and gain readers. Adeline and I have plans to celebrate in Austin this weekend, splurging on a hotel for a night to enjoy ourselves. Not only because it's my tenth book, but because I'm *this close* to sales on my books finally reaching the same amount of money I bring home from the rodeo every month.

I'm salivating at the vision of handing in my resignation. The plan is once I reach that figure that secures my freedom, Adeline and I will move to Austin permanently. She currently works for her father at his car dealership and fortunately, he has another one twenty minutes from downtown Austin that he said she can transfer to. I'm realistic in the sense that I don't think this book will push me over the edge to hand in my resignation next week. But I have two more books lined up after this one and if I can keep the momentum up, I should be able to say adios to Bear Creek Rodeo forever.

Distractions in my life right now are non-negotiable.

No partying.

No men.

*Nothing!*

"Tessa, I'm ready for our meeting," Mr. George calls out from his office, disrupting me from my thoughts. With the rodeo one month away, Mr. George likes to have daily meetings to go over what we've accomplished to make sure we're ready without any hitches for the big weekend. Considering we've been doing this for so long, I find it comical that I'm still being micromanaged. I've stopped letting it bother me since a new chapter in my life is about to come to fruition. I owe a lot to Mr. George for taking pity on me that day, which now feels like forever ago. I've forgiven Ty for his wrongdoings because if it wasn't for my experience with him, I wouldn't be where I am today:

*An up-and-coming successful romance author!*

I can't help the smile that plays on my lips as I walk into Mr. George's office and sit down. My smile must be extra bright today, because normally Mr. George doesn't pay much attention to me, but today he does a double take and stares at me.

"I haven't seen you smile like that for a long time. What's on that mind of yours? You've got a hot date tonight, Tessa?" He raises his eyebrows in question and I can't help but giggle at the hope that's in his eyes. He's been my boss now for seven years and sometimes I feel he views me as the daughter he never had.

"I don't need any man to make me smile, sir. So to answer your question, no, I don't have a hot date tonight. Can't a girl just be happy?" No one except Adeline and my other friend, Kendall, know of my alter ego and I plan to keep it that way. People talk and I don't need anyone derailing me.

He shakes his head and laughs. "I'm glad that you can make yourself happy, Tessa, but aren't you interested in anyone? You're a beautiful, smart, young lady. Don't you want to settle down soon?"

"Nope," I say, popping the "p" to emphasize my point.

He leans back in his chair and studies me for a second. "You know you broke Scottie's heart last week when you told him hell would have to freeze over for you to ever go out on a date with him."

I tap my finger on my lips and look upward, remembering my version of the story to be quite different then what Mr. George was told. "If I recall correctly, Scottie never formally asked me out on a date. He asked me if I wanted to feel what it's like for a horse to be ridden by the best bareback bronc rider in Texas." Mr. George's mouth drops open in shock, his cheeks turning red from embarrassment and his eyes hardening in disgust.

"That man shouldn't be allowed to compete. That's sexual harassment and is unacceptable at my rodeo." Mr. George reaches for the phone, but I stop him by holding up my hand.

"With all due respect, Mr. George, I don't want the demise of his career on my conscience. I also don't want the gossip. As you well know, this town talks, especially if it has to do with one of the cowboys." He nods in agreements, knowing all too well how this town loves to hear about any gossip concerning the rodeo and the professional cowboys that ride here.

"Next time you have any kind of incident with anyone, I want to hear about it. You understand, Tessa?" I nod and return his intense stare so that he knows I hear him loud and clear. "Good, let's get down to business."

We go through our master list of things that need to be ready. As usual, we're sitting pretty with having most of our tasks completed. If the rodeo started tomorrow, we would be in great shape. All that would be missing would be the cowboys since they usually report the day of. If we're lucky, they will come the night before and attend our annual carnival and sign autographs. We're ready to go and the only reason I can think why Mr. George is nervous might be due to the new addition of cowboys that are gracing us with their presence this rodeo season.

The Kearney brothers from Ireland.

I don't know much about them except for what I've read in the media, which is that they're taking the rodeo circuit by storm. They've already obtained more sponsors than some cowboys could only dream of having. Rodeos are selling out and people are driving all over the state to attend multiple rodeos just to see them. Word on the street is that they're professional, on time, and show great sportsmanship.

And that they're more handsome than any other cowboy in the history of the PRCA.

Ty is still the best-looking cowboy I've ever seen here in Bear Creek, but that isn't saying much. I've never been to the National Finals in Las Vegas, so I find it hard to believe that the gossip of the Kearney brothers being the hottest cowboys ever could be true. They're listed as single and according to Adeline, no girlfriends have been reported or spotted at any of the rodeos they've competed in so far.

Not that I care about any of this gossip. Whether they're good-looking or not won't phase me since I have no plans on shacking up with a professional cowboy ever again.

"I think we need to beef up security for the Kearney boys. One of the other general managers from another rodeo sent out an email saying they had a hard time controlling the pack of ladies who tried following them to the dressing room."

I roll my eyes at this news, not understanding why some women are so desperate. I jot down to hire more cops on my task list for tomorrow.

"I'll order more officers, but I feel we're prepared for them just like we're prepared for all the other cowboys who compete in Bear Creek Rodeo." I don't want my boss to put these guys on a pedestal. We can't be accused of having favorites and catering to some cowboys more than others.

"With the way they're performing, Tessa, I think we're going to see history in the making. Try to reach out to their team to see if we can persuade them to come early. I want them to be at our press conference with the rest of the cowboys, as well as signing autographs at the carnival. We're blessed to be sold out again and we still have some standing room only tickets left. What do you think of the idea of maybe getting a big screen and doing a watch party outside the arena for those who didn't get a ticket before we sold out?"

"I think it's a great idea," I respond with fake enthusiasm, knowing full well that my opinion won't matter to Mr. George. He's going to do it no matter what I think.

"Excellent. Order a screen and lets schedule a meeting with ground operations to get this in motion. Once we figure out logistics, let's announce our plan to the media."

I nod, but am inwardly groaning at the fact that Mr. George already plans on making a big deal of the Kearney brothers being in Bear Creek, which means extra work for me.

*Please let this be my final rodeo,* I silently pray.

I'm done catering to these entitled cowboys.

# Chapter 3

## RHETT

"CAN WE PLEASE stop for dinner soon? I'm starving!" Ryan whines while I drive us down Highway 35 in Texas to our next destination.

The road life that comes with the territory of being a professional cowboy is starting to take its toll. It's been seven months now since we left Ireland for America and most of the time, I can't even remember what state we're in. The schedule here is much more grueling than in Australia. We travel to another new rodeo almost every other day with no rest in between. If we aren't driving, then we're flying, but flying is expensive, so most of the time we're renting cars. We're the rookies of the circuit, so Ryan and I agreed to go hardcore and try to hit up every rodeo that qualifies us for Nationals. Now I question whether that was a wise decision. We're running on fumes, which affects our concentration and how we perform. I can't wait for the break before Finals. The light is at the end of the tunnel since we have one more month left, but if we do this again next year, we must do things differently.

"We have only thirty minutes left until we reach the hotel. Can you wait or are you going to pass out on me like a pansy?" I look in my rearview mirror at Ryan, who decided to take a nap in the back seat.

"Fine," he grumbles, not liking the idea of having to wait. "We need to strategize this better for next year. I'm fucking tired."

"I was just thinking the same thing," I smile while glancing back at him. There's no way we can sustain this type of schedule and dominate the pro rodeo circuit. "Let's talk more at dinner about how we're going to maximize our winnings by which rodeos we choose and how to minimize our traveling expenses for next year." Thank goodness we secured some sponsors because their sponsorship money helps pay for our travel. Taking that year off to take care of the farm also helped us save money since our experiences in Australia and Spain were similar and we had somewhat of an idea of what to expect.

"Hey, are we near Austin?" Ryan asks as we pass a sign on the highway that says we're ten miles away from it. "Cody just sent me a text saying they're eating dinner downtown and that if we're close, we should join them. Can we? We've been snotty pricks by not socializing with anyone so far."

We've kept to ourselves this tour simply because we don't know who to trust. We've heard plenty of stories of who the assholes of the circuit are, but I like to be my own judge of character. We've noticed the cliques and with us being fresh meat, some of the other cowboys haven't been so welcoming. Cody Burr took it upon himself to try to help us anytime we're at the same rodeo together. It would be nice to have a beer with him, buy his dinner as a thank you, and pick his brain on what we should do for next year.

"You're right, we should stop and take him up on his offer. Find out where he is so I can put it into the navigation."

Thirty minutes later we're walking into a restaurant on 6th Street. The restaurant is packed, but Cody and his friends stick out with their cowboy hats on. Ryan and I never wear our hats outside the rodeo. Even though Ryan is the louder and more obnoxious one of us, we both agree that we don't like to draw attention to ourselves. We make our way through the crowd to the bar where Cody and his crew are sitting.

"Holy crap, I didn't recognize you two. You look like total hipsters instead of cowboys. Where's your hats?" Cody comments as soon as he turns around after I tap him on his shoulder. He's with three other cowboys from the circuit—Tate Reynolds, Luke Reno, and Casey Jennings. All three men are a force on the circuit and have been respectful to Ryan and me every time we compete with them.

"We don't wear our hats when we aren't competing," Ryan responds while shaking hands with the other guys.

"Well, you should. The ladies here love them some cowboys." Casey tips his hat down to salute a pretty redhead that passes us by. She gives him a sly smile in return while continuing to her table. "See what I mean?" he laughs and signals for the bartender. We place our order and while we wait for our drinks, I decide to look around.

The restaurant's decor is a mixture of country farmhouse meets rustic industrial with a few crystal chandeliers to glam it up. The Friday night crowd is lively and I imagine it's probably like this every weekend. My eyes slowly travel over the tables in front of us, casually roaming until I do a double take at the sight of a beautiful brunette.

Her smile is mesmerizing while she laughs at something her friend is saying. It's the type of smile that you automatically smile back at, even if she isn't looking at you. It's genuine, with her skin crinkling at the side of her eyes that are shining brightly from happiness. As I watch her more closely, I can actually hear her whimsical laughter.

And I want to hear more of it.

A glass of Guinness is slapped into my chest, shaking me out of my thoughts and causing me to look away. It's been a very long time since I've been interested in someone, so maybe that's why I'm reacting so strongly to this stranger. No doubt she's gorgeous, but so are other women in this place. I continue to people watch, but can't stop my gaze from wandering back to her.

She's listening intently to whatever her friend is saying, her smile fading into a look of disbelief. Her friend, who's a cute, petite blonde with long hair, is talking rapidly, her voice getting louder and louder with excitement over whatever she's looking at on her phone. She shoves her phone into the brunette's face, who looks at it in shock. Her blonde friend starts banging on their table with both of her hands, her voice getting loud enough for me to understand what she's saying.

"You have a freaking orange flag!" she yells out and then screams in delight. The brunette quickly looks up from her phone, telling her friend to be quiet. She looks around and apologizes to the people at the table next to them for her friend's loudness.

*What in the hell is an orange flag for?*

"Rhett! Are you listening to us?" Ryan's voice brings my attention back to him, but only for half a second as I try to acknowledge him while still keeping my eyes on her.

"Clearly someone else has his attention. Who are you looking at?" All four of them follow my line of vision and for a second, I wish they hadn't just seen my diamond in the rough.

"Tate, doesn't the brunette look familiar?" Cody asks out loud and my heart starts to sink at the thought that one of them has dated her already. I have a strict rule to not be with anyone who has dated someone I know. This rule is non-negotiable and fortunately, I've never been in a position to even consider breaking it.

"She does look familiar. I bet she's a buckle bunny." Buckle bunny is code for groupie. Disappointment starts to fill me, hoping they're wrong. She hasn't looked our way once. If she was a rodeo groupie, wouldn't she try hanging out with us?

*Why does this even matter, Rhett? You can't commit to anyone right now anyway, plus this girl could be a psychopath.*

"Ah, I remember now! She works at Bear Creek Rodeo. Her name is ... Tessa! Tessa Mandel! She's Caldwell George's assistant," Tate confirms and relief washes through me knowing she isn't a groupie. "I wouldn't get your sights set on her, Kearney. She makes it crystal clear to any man who even comes near her that she isn't interested."

I smile at this, loving the fact that she doesn't get involved with people at the rodeo. There must be a reason for this as someone like Tessa probably gets hit on daily working at a place like that.

"Ryan, is Bear Creek Rodeo on our schedule?" I ask over my shoulder, keeping my eyes trained on her. If it wasn't before, it will be now as my brain is screaming to go talk to her. There's something about Tessa Mandel. Something ... *special*.

"Yes, it's on our schedule," Ryan confirms, amusement lacing his voice as he knows exactly what his big brother is up to. She doesn't look like a psycho—in fact, she looks more like an angel. An angel I want to get to know better.

"I think it might be best if I go introduce myself to Miss Mandel ahead of time." I turn around and wink at the boys, who slap me on my back with encouragement.

"Want my hat?" Casey offers his cowboy hat to me, which I politely decline while putting my beer down on the bar.

"I don't need a cowboy hat to get a woman," I declare and turn my back on the hooting and hollering that is coming from the boys. With my heart pounding, I slowly walk over and pray that the intuition buzzing through my body is right.

That this woman was made to be mine.

# Chapter 4

## TESSA

I SIT BACK in my seat in shock, still not able to digest what I saw by the title of my latest book release.

That coveted orange flag.

That flag that signifies my book is #1 in one of the categories that it's listed in on one of the biggest book platforms in the world.

That flag signifies that I'm a best-selling author.

That flag signifies I'm one step closer to my dreams of becoming a reality.

"How much money do you think you're making right now?" Adeline asks, her eyes bright with happiness for me. For us, because without her support and push, I honestly don't know if I would be where I'm at today.

"I don't know. Just because I'm #1 in a category doesn't mean it's bringing me sales."

"You're ranked in the top 100 in the whole entire store. Do you understand that? Top 100 out of millions of books!"

I stare at her, blinking occasionally as I try to digest her words.

That's the lowest rank I've ever gotten in my entire career and this is only day one of release week. There's a chance my rank will go lower.

"That's it, Tessa, we're celebrating. We're getting rip roaring drunk and eating whatever the hell we want. We deserve to celebrate!" Adeline practically yells, waving at our waiter to get his attention. I laugh with her, because her excitement is contagious and damnit, I do deserve to celebrate. *We* deserve to celebrate since this means our dreams of getting out of Bear Creek will be happening as soon as the rodeo is over with. The wheels in my head start turning as we have a lot to do, starting with finding an apartment in Austin. All of this can wait because I need to live in the present and celebrate this moment. I take out my phone and search for my book, taking a screenshot of it with the flag. I then take a screenshot of my ranking. When the waiter comes around with our flutes of champagne, I put my phone away and raise my glass for Adeline's toast.

"To Tessa, my best friend, my inspiration, my sister from another mister! Congratulations to you on this huge accomplishment! You're going to be an international best-selling badass author babe and I'm honored to be your forever assistant." I laugh, because knowing Adeline, she *will be* my forever assistant. "Thank you for having me on this journey with you and never doubt your self-worth. You deserve all of this and more!"

"I love you, Adeline Murphy. Thank you for always believing in me and we deserve this!" I smile through the tears that threaten to leak out of my eyes as we clink our glasses together and drink. I put my glass down and start to rapidly blink, praying that I don't start crying in the middle of the restaurant. I look around to see if anyone is watching us when my eyes land on the hottest guy I've ever seen.

*And he's coming straight toward me!*

My breath hitches in my chest when his smile ignites the flapping of butterfly wings in my stomach. My brain, wanting to see more of him, directs my eyes up and down his body. His dark blond hair is buzzed on the sides and spiked on the top, his black t-shirt stretching nicely across his muscular body. His dark denim jeans are like gloves over his tight thighs and he's wearing black boots.

And for once they're not cowboy boots.

This man oozes sex appeal and I'm not the only woman whose eyes are drawn to him like magnets. Heads are turning his way as he inches closer and closer to our table.

*Breathe, Tessa! He's just a guy probably coming to talk to Adeline.*

I try to calm my breathing down and glance at Adeline to see if she has noticed him yet, but she is busy looking at her phone. I'm about to whisper her name to get her attention when out of the corner of my eye, I see him standing next to me. My eyes meet his, my lips parting at the beauty of their color—bright, emerald green.

"Excuse me ladies for interrupting your dinner, but I had to meet the woman who has the most beautiful smile I've ever seen and a laugh that is music to my soul."

I stare at him with wide eyes, waiting for that disdain feeling of disgust to overcome me at his corny pick-up line, but instead I'm mesmerized by his low, husky voice with an accent that is clearly foreign and not from this country. I continue to stare at him, feeling the heat stain my cheeks red while I look at his full lips, wondering what those lips would feel like against mine.

*Wait, what?*

"Tessa, aren't you going to say thank you to this kind gentleman?" Adeline chides, looking at me as if I'm some crazy lunatic.

*If she only knew that I feel like a crazy lunatic with the kind of thoughts I'm having over a complete stranger.*

"Right," I clear my throat from the dryness he has caused and shake my head, hoping to get control over myself. "I'm sorry … and um, thanks."

For a best-selling author, I'm a bumbling idiot right now.

"No, I'm sorry, I sounded like a total creeper just now. What I meant to say is that your beauty and laughter caught my attention and I just had to come over to say hello. Also, I heard your friend say in excitement something about an orange flag and your reaction to it was priceless. So, what does an orange flag mean?" He cocks his head to the side in curiosity and I can't help but bite my lip at how damn adorable he looks doing it.

And hot.

And sexy.

And I'm in trouble.

*Get control of yourself, Tessa! This man is a complete stranger and could even be a serial killer.*

*No distractions!*

I look over at Adeline, her brown eyes twinkling in amusement at my sorry state. She raises her eyebrows at me, daring me to tell him the truth since she knows I want my author life kept private.

"An orange flag is what the referees throw out at football games," I pathetically reply, my brain still not in its full, functioning state. *How stupid did that just sound?* I couldn't think of an answer fast enough and I'm just not ready to tell a complete stranger my news.

His eyes light up in amusement, his lips moving into a wicked smirk. Laughter rumbles out of him, causing me to tighten my legs together and clench my core muscles at how delicious it sounds. "If I'm not mistaken, it's a yellow flag that they throw in American football games." I refrain from closing my eyes and sighing at the sound of his voice. I could listen to this man talk every minute of every hour for the rest of my life.

*What in the hell is wrong me?*

"Oh for crying out loud, Tessa! He's harmless!" Adeline clucks her tongue at me as if I'm a chicken. She gives Mr. International Hottie her undivided attention, ignoring me when I tap my foot against her shin in warning. "This amazing woman right here is an author and an orange flag means she's a best-selling one to boot!"

This time I spare her no mercy and kick her shin hard underneath the table. Her eyes widen in pain and then narrow at me, telling me I will pay for that later.

"Wow, you're an author? That's remarkable. Congratulations!" he says with sincerity, looking at me with even more interest. "What type of author are you?"

"I write romance books," I mumble, too embarrassed to look him in the eyes when I tell him that. I have nothing to be ashamed about, but for some reason, I don't want to see any ridicule coming from him.

"Do you write from experience?" My head snaps up to look at him to see if he's mocking me. His eyes are intense, the seriousness in his voice making me believe that he wouldn't make fun of me for writing the type of books I write.

"No, I don't," I answer, shocked at my honesty. "I like to write other people's happy endings."

"And what about your own?" He inches closer to me, holding my gaze so intently that I couldn't look away even if I wanted to. I gulp down the huge lump that is stuck in my throat, wishing I had the power to tell this man to leave me alone even though I don't want him to.

"I haven't had mine yet," I finally respond, my answer rewarding me with another one of his beautiful smiles.

"Good."

*Good? What in the world does that mean?*

"What's your name, Miss Best-Selling Author?" I can't stop the giggle that bubbles up at his compliment while I shake his awaiting hand. My fingers rub up against his calloused palm and I wonder what he does for a living to have such rough hands. His firm, warm grip has my mind envisioning his hands roaming other parts of my body. I quickly retract those thoughts, trying to re-focus my attention to his question.

"Her name is Tessa. What's your name, Mr. Sexy Foreigner?"

Adeline answers for me and for one moment, I forgot that she was even there. For him to make me forget my best friend's presence is a sure sign that this man is dangerous for my mental state.

"So wait, you *are* Tessa Mandel?" he asks, giving me a puzzling look and I immediately freeze, not understanding how he knows me.

*How does some stranger in Austin know who I am?*

"How do you know my last name?" I question, looking at Adeline for any clues, but she looks just as confused as I am.

"My buddies over there know you. Said you work for Bear Creek Rodeo. You are an author and work at the rodeo?" I look around him to see three familiar faces watching our interaction. All three of them wave and give me a thumbs up, acting as if I'm their little sister and they're playing matchmaker.

*Crap!*

"Yes, I work at the rodeo," I groan, my excitement turning to nervousness at the news that this guy knows Tate, Luke, and Casey. I don't need to be with anyone who knows those three. Cowboys gossip just as badly as girls do and I refuse to be the talk of the dressing room, nor do I want Mr. George finding out about my alter ego. I grip his hand tighter and cover our hands with my free one. "Please, they don't know I'm a writer. Please don't say anything," I plead with him, my eyes begging for his silence.

He studies me for a long second before responding. "Your secret is safe with me, Tessa." He squeezes my hand back and I remove it from his just as Tate and the rest of the boys come up to our table.

"Fancy seeing you here, Tessa. I see you've met our new friend," Tate says, throwing his arm around Mr. Sexy Foreigner's shoulders. My ears perk up at the word "new". If this is a new friend to them, then there's a chance he's not close with them … yet. Hope makes me sit up straighter in my chair. Maybe I can persuade him to not hang out with cowboys, especially at rodeos. He doesn't even look like he would hang out with them with the way he dresses. Although his clothes are simple, they look expensive. Austin's a big music town, so maybe he's a musician or in the music business.

"Where did you two meet?" I ask, but out of the corner of my eye, I see some other stranger introducing himself to Adeline. He's also very handsome and as I look at little bit closer, he's wearing the same type of clothing as Mr. Sexy Foreigner.

*What in the hell is going on here?*

"Tessa, do you not realize who you're talking to?" Tate asks me, but Mr. Sexy Foreigner shakes his head at him.

"No, we were at introductions when you so rudely interrupted." I don't mean to be a bitch to Tate since he is actually one of the nicer guys on the tour. In fact, him, Casey and Luke all have been nice to me, never once trying to hit on me or make me feel uncomfortable. I immediately regret my tone of voice with him, but I wish it was just me alone with my sexy stranger now.

*Since when did he become mine?*

"Well, let's not waste another minute longer. Tessa, this is Gerard Butler. Gerard, Tessa Mandel." Everyone laughs at his joke because clearly, Mr. Sexy Foreigner looks nothing like Gerard Butler.

"Personally, I think I should be the one called Gerard Butler since I have his coloring more than my brother does. I'm referring to the younger, buff Gerard Butler in the movie *300*;" The other sexy stranger winks at Adeline, his accent just like Mr. Sexy Foreigner's. He has dark brown hair and is smaller in build, but when he looks my way, I gasp at the same emerald green eyes.

Brothers.

With an accent that I can only assume is Irish.

"In all seriousness, Tessa, you've been talking to *the* Irish Cowboy this whole time! I know you know who I'm talking about now, right?"

"Just because Gerard Butler played an Irish man in *P.S. I Love You* doesn't make him Irish. He's Scottish, you jackasses,"

Adeline scolds in her signature sassy tone, shaking her head at Tate's mistake.

While the guys debate about the heritage of Gerard Butler, my gaze travels back to Mr. Sexy Foreigner and my stomach starts to ache at the knowledge that this was all too good to be true. *Of course he has to be a cowboy!* Why couldn't fate for once put someone that wasn't one in my path? Sadness starts to wash over me like a slow, steady mist of rain. I've never reacted to a stranger like this before and for a brief instant, I thought maybe I found someone that was special.

*Why couldn't he be different?*

*Why did he have to be a cowboy?*

I've never had a good poker face, so I feel the disappointment settle into me. It's hard for me to even look him in the eyes anymore. I know he senses the change in me and with most guys, they would get the hint. But it seems like Mr. Sexy Foreigner is anything but ordinary. He places one hand on the back of my chair and the other hand on the table. He leans down, bringing his face only inches from mine, his lips hovering close to my ear.

"Let me formally introduce myself to you because this moment is one I don't want you to ever forget. My name is Rhett Kearney and you'll soon be typing 'The End' to your singlehood once you realize that I'm going to be your happily ever after."

## Chapter 5

### RHETT

WHAT I SAID to Tessa was the ballsiest thing I've ever said to a woman. Scratch that, the *craziest* thing I've ever said to a woman. How can I tell a woman I just met that I'm going to be her endgame? But when I saw her demeanor completely change once she realized who I was, I had to do and say something drastic in order to get her attention back. The idea is crazy, but for some reason, the words felt so right. I rendered her speechless to the point that she stayed quiet the rest of the evening.

At Adeline's invitation, we joined the girls at their table, ordered food and continued talking. Tessa made small talk when needed, but for the most part, she sat quietly in her chair, silently brooding over my declaration while continuing to imbibe more alcohol. I switched to water once it was apparent that she was drinking her emotions, the roller coaster ride she was on written all over her face. Adeline, being the astute best friend that she is, also switched to water and continued to monitor her friend when Ryan didn't have her undivided attention. Ryan was talking Adeline's ear off, which isn't his normal mode of operation when picking up women. Usually it's the women talking off his ear and while they're doing that, he's assessing whether he's taking them home or not.

My attention is brought back to Tessa, who's half listening to a story Casey is telling about his most recent performance. Any time Bear Creek is mentioned, her lips curl slightly in disgust. *What has happened at Bear Creek to make her feel so negatively about it?* When she isn't listening to someone talking, she's staring off into space. I know my words are still having an effect on her because when she thinks I'm not looking, I catch her staring at me, looking at me as if we're in a faraway place alone in her mind. What I wouldn't give right now to know what's going on in that gorgeous head of hers.

The chemistry between us was electrifying and we haven't even physically touched each other besides a handshake. Despite the desire that I saw in her earlier, I can tell Tessa is going to be resistant to giving me a chance. Something has happened in her past for her to have this thick wall of ice up around her heart. But I'm always up for a challenge and from what I can see so far, Tessa Mandel is worth fighting for.

Besides her outside beauty, Tessa has showed that she's smart, has character, is strong-minded, and has a fire burning bright inside her to make something of herself. For her to have a secret career as an author on the side tells me she wants more than what she has at Bear Creek Rodeo. Her disdain for cowboys, whom she's around 24/7, proves her plans don't include relying on a man to get what she wants. The love I saw shining through her eyes at her best friend before I interrupted their celebration tells me that when she loves hard, she loves fiercely.

And that's exactly the kind of love I've been looking for.

Just like I have to prove myself to the world that I'm the best bronc rider within eight-seconds, I'm going to have to prove myself to Tessa that I'm sincerely interested in being with her.

And my actions are going to be the way to her heart.

I continue listening to the conversation, enjoying everyone's company, when I notice Tessa's eyes have become glossy. Her eyelids start to droop and I know it isn't long before she is going to fall asleep at the table. Ryan now has Adeline fully engaged in conversation, so I remove myself from my chair and kneel down next to Tessa.

"Little lass, are you ready to go to bed?" I softly ask, wondering how far the drive to her house in Bear Creek is from here. We can always get a hotel here for her to sleep it off if need be.

Her head bobs to the side, the alcohol now affecting her motor movements. She half smiles/half sneers at me as she tries wagging her finger in my face. "You can take those thoughts and shove it, as there's no way I'll be going to bed tonight with you, sir. I don't go to bed with strangers. You, my sexy foreigner, are going to bed all by yourself tonight and your hand can keep your lower brain company."

I throw my head back and laugh at how hilarious and adorable drunk Tessa is. My heart swells with pride that although she admitted I'm sexy, she doesn't jump right into bed with people she just meets.

"Thank you for those explicit instructions, but that isn't what I meant. I only meant sleep and nothing more ... that is until you're ready to share a bed with me." I lick my lips at the images that come to mind of Tessa in my bed, naked and ready for me.

"Oh," she says sheepishly while trying to get her eyes focused on me. "Yes, I think sleep might be a good idea right now."

"Adeline," I command loud enough to get her attention away from Ryan. Her eyes widen as she takes in the condition of her friend. "How far away is Tessa's house? She needs to go to sleep."

"We have a hotel room for tonight and it's only a block away. Do you mind helping me get her there?" she asks while she stands up and Ryan moves her chair back out of the way for her.

"It was always my plan to make sure you two got home safely." I rise and help Tessa out of her chair. She gets to her feet fine, but as soon as I let go of her arm, she starts to wobble.

"Whoa lass, I've got you." I wrap my arm around her waist and pull her to my side. She grabs onto my shirt and looks up at me, her dark blue eyes staring at my mouth. Her lashes are painted with mascara but I can still tell they are naturally long. I have a hard time believing there is anything fake about this girl.

"You have very nice lips. If you weren't a cowboy, I would kiss them," she tells me and I softly groan at how uncomfortable the tightness in my pants have gotten. I have every intention of kissing Tessa—when she's ready and begging for it.

"I'll quit the rodeo tomorrow if it means I get a taste of you," I whisper in her ear. Her cheeks flare red and her eyes widen when she sees how serious I am. Before she looks down, I catch the same spark of desire that I saw earlier from her when she didn't know who I was.

Adeline moves to Tessa's other side to help balance her upright. Ryan carries the girls' purses for them and we bid farewell to the other guys. We walk that one block to the hotel and as soon as we get in the elevator, Tessa wraps her arms around me and lays her head against my chest. My arms instinctively wrap tighter around her and I rest my chin on top of her head. She fits perfectly in my arms, as if she was made to be there. I close my eyes and I can picture us in the same position, standing on a balcony, watching the ocean.

When I hear the ding of the elevator, I open my eyes and see Adeline and Ryan staring at us, a weird expression crossing both of their faces. The doors to the elevator open and I scoop Tessa up into my arms so that I can carry her safely into her hotel room.

"Wait, I've got to get a picture of this for blackmail purposes," Adeline laughs as she gets her phone out of her purse that Ryan was carrying for her and snaps a photo of me holding Tessa. She leads us to their room and opens the door for me. I lay Tessa on the bed closest to the bathroom since she might need it in the middle of the night. Adeline starts taking off Tessa's shoes and as I stare down at Tessa, a strong need to stay with them overcomes me. I don't want to overstep my boundaries and I know Adeline will take the very best care of her. Besides, Tessa seems to have a lot of pride and I doubt she'll want me to see her in the morning after a rough night. I bet she'll already be embarrassed by her inebriation.

I kneel down beside the bed and push Tessa's hair off her face. She's exquisite even in her sleep. Her long lashes sweep against the tops of her rosy cheeks. Her lips part slightly as she exhales out.

"Good night, little lass. I'll see you tomorrow," I whisper and as I stand upright, her eyelids flutter open and she looks at me.

"Am I dreaming right now?" she asks, making me chuckle at the awe in her voice as she looks me up and down.

"No, lass, you're not. Ryan and I are leaving and we just wanted to make sure you girls got to the hotel okay." She grabs hold of my hand and tugs, making me bend down closer to her. I try to gently disengage her hands from me, but her grip is surprisingly strong for someone so drunk. "Do you want me to stay, lass?"

"No, I want you to stay *away* from me." She stares at me for a couple of seconds before smiling and closing her eyes. Her grip loosens and she lets go of me.

"I'm never going to stay away from you, Tessa Mandel. Start getting used to it."

She sighs and for a moment, I think she's asleep before she surprises me with her next words. "We'll see. All men run away." And with that, she rolls away to the opposite side of the bed.

I want to kill whoever broke her heart. But then, we wouldn't be here together if he hadn't.

"Adeline, can you please give me her phone number?" I ask and with the way Adeline is staring so intensely at me, I feel she isn't going to do it. Whatever internal battle she's having with herself ends and she grabs the pen and paper out of the nightstand drawer.

"Hurt my friend and I'll personally poison the next beer you drink," she threatens, looking at me dead in the eyes with ferocity. I wouldn't put it passed Adeline to kill for Tessa. Their love and loyalty for each other is evident.

"Rest assured, I'll never intentionally hurt Tessa," I state as I grab the piece of paper out of Adeline's hands. "Thank you for this. I'll call her in the morning."

"Fair warning, she might not pick up. Tessa is pretty adamant about not getting involved with cowboys." She sighs and moves toward the door, indicating she's ready for us to leave.

"Hey, where's my digits?" Ryan whines as we follow her to the door. I've never heard my brother sound more pathetic asking for a girl's phone number. It makes me want to slap him upside the head right now, but I refrain. In fact, Ryan is usually not the one asking for phone numbers. Girls slip him their digits all the time, even when he doesn't ask for it.

"You didn't properly ask for it, so therefore, you don't get it." Adeline smiles sweetly at him, making me chuckle at her brazenness while I walk past her into the hallway.

"You're a sassy one ... and I like it!" Ryan looks her up and down in appreciation, which causes Adeline to roll her eyes. He wiggles his eyebrows up and down and that actually makes her giggle. It's exactly the reaction he was hoping to get out of her.

"You better start getting used to seeing me around as well, Sassy." Ryan swoops in and manages to sneak a kiss on her cheek before he walks out into the hallway.

"We'll see if both of you are men enough to prove it."

And with that, she slams the door in our faces.

## Chapter 6

### TESSA

I CAN COUNT on one hand the times I've thrown up in my life and about three of those times happened within the last 24 hours alone. Fortunately, I made it to the bathroom each time, with Adeline beside me to hold my hair back. Each time she helped clean me up and put me right back to bed. I hate losing control of myself like that. Normally when I drink, I make sure I've eaten plenty of food and drink water in between beverages. But, for some reason, I was consumed with drinking my sorrows away about Rhett being a cowboy. The one guy that sparks a fire in me since Ty and he had to be what I've sworn off.

I deserved the way I felt today, guilt eating at me with the fact that Adeline had to take care of me as if I were a baby. As soon as I woke up, she was awake with water and aspirin for my headache. I took a hot shower, got dressed, and we checked out of the hotel. Halfway back to Bear Creek, we stopped for breakfast. I was ravenous and the grease from my potatoes and eggs actually helped my stomach.

"Have you checked your phone yet?" she inquires in between

bites of her breakfast. I look up at her, my eyes questioning why as I chewed my food. "To see if Rhett called," she says in her "duh" kind of voice.

I swallow the chunk of food and shake my head. "I didn't give him my phone number so how could he call?"

"I gave him your phone number!" she says in exasperation.

"Why would you do that? You know I won't date cowboys." Considering that Adeline was with me on the anti-cowboy movement, it's surprising that she would've given him my number.

"I gave him your phone number because he wasn't going to leave our hotel room without it and I've never seen you react toward a man like the way you did to him."

I shrug my shoulders nonchalantly, trying to make light of it, when in fact my heart is racing at the knowledge that he wanted my phone number. "My reaction was just lust. He *is* quite good-looking after all."

"Cut the bullcrap, Tessa—this is me you're talking to. You felt something way more than lust for him. He rattled you."

I put down my fork and look her straight in the eyes. "Yeah, he rattled me, okay? In the most uncomfortable, yet delicious way. How can a stranger evict such intense feelings out of me? It's got to be just from lack of attention."

"Tessa, you get hit on all the time at the rodeo, so you can't say it's from lack of attention. There's a reason you reacted the way you did. Maybe he's the one?" My eyebrows shoot up in disbelief that she just uttered those words.

"I think you've read too many love stories, Adeline. Besides, he's exactly the type of person I don't want to date."

"Who cares if he's a cowboy, Tessa! Not all cowboys are the same. Not all men just want to get laid and move on." Sometimes I think Adeline would've made a great lawyer with the way she argues. She's passionate and always believes she's right.

"Let's say he is one of the good guys, there's still a huge strike against him. He lives in Ireland!" I throw down my napkin, the topic of conversation making me lose my appetite.

"Soooo?" she asks slowly, not even acting as if this is an issue.

"So you want me to move to Ireland?" I counter back, having a hard time believing she would be willing to give-up our dream of moving to Austin together.

"If it means you're in love and with the right person, then yes, I would want you to move to Ireland. It would suck and I would miss you, but your happiness is everything to me." She reaches across the table and squeezes my hand. "Listen, Tessa. What Ty did was beyond horrible, but most men are not assholes like him. You've got to stop assuming that all men are going to hurt you the way he did. Is it possible you might get hurt again in the future? Of course it's possible. But missing out on any kind of love would be the biggest shame of it all." She gives my hand one last squeeze. "You've got to believe that you deserve your happily ever after too and the only way you can get one is giving someone a chance."

I contemplate her words while we wait for the check. It isn't that I disagree with her, I just don't know if Rhett Kearney is the right person to be open-minded about. When the check arrives, I pay for our meal and we get back on the road.

"Out of all the men you know have shown interest in me, why do you think I should give Rhett a chance?" I ask once we've been on the road for a while. The more I think about it, the more I'm convinced that Rhett would be the wrong person to take a chance on due to his current living situation.

"I think he's the perfect person to dip your toe back in the dating waters with and here's why. One; it was obvious to everyone in that restaurant that you two are extremely attracted to each other. I swear there was one point where I think you both forgot about everyone around you." I blush slightly at her words and look out the window because that's exactly what happened.

"Two; he made it pretty clear last night that he wasn't giving up until you did give him a chance."

"Actions speak louder than words though," I respond, something that I've preached since Ty's deception. Words are powerful, but following them up with action is what proves someone's sincerity to me.

"But if you don't give them a chance, how can they prove it to you with their actions?" she debates and I hate to admit it, but she does have a point.

"And lastly; if things don't work out between the two of you, he goes back to Ireland. Since this will be your last rodeo, you won't run the risk of ever running into him again." It's easy for Adeline to say that—she's never been in love before. She doesn't know what it's like to have your heart broken and shattered into a million pieces. She's always cutting guys loose before she has a chance to fall for them. She says it's because she knew right away that she wasn't going to be in love with them. I have a hard time believing that since she doesn't give herself a chance to fall in love.

Regardless, all of her advice is just words because she's never experienced heartache.

"Have you checked your phone yet?" she asks again when we pull into the parking lot of our apartment. I shake my head and rummage through my purse to find it.

"It's dead. I'll charge it when we get upstairs."

We get out of the car and into our apartment. I plug my phone into the charger in the kitchen and go into my bedroom, where I immediately lie down and fall asleep.

And dream of one sexy, Irish Cowboy.

## Chapter 7

### RHETT

"WHEN ARE YOU going to quit leaving her messages?" Ryan asks after I hang up the phone from trying to reach Tessa again. Even though Adeline warned me, I was hoping she would be wrong and that Tessa would've picked up on the first ring.

Four messages later and not only has Tessa not picked up, but she still hasn't called me back.

"Until she picks up," I respond, not willing to give up that easily on her. My feelings last night were too strong to ignore and just brush aside. "I wish you got Adeline's phone number so we could call her to make sure everything's okay."

"I'm sure everything is fine and Tessa doesn't want to talk to you because you're proving to be a creepy stalker. You're sure starting to creep *me* out. I've never seen you react this way over a girl."

I chuckle at him and think maybe he's right—I need to stop calling her. At least maybe wait until tomorrow.

"There's something special about her, Ryan. I can feel it. Until she tells me personally that she never wants to hear from me again, I'm not giving up." I look him dead in the eye so he can see how serious I am about her.

"C'mon, let's go work out so we're ready for Belton this weekend," I suggest, needing some sort of distraction to take my mind off of Tessa. The rodeo in Belton is an hour and fifteen minutes away from Bear Creek. After Belton, we travel north for a couple of rodeos closer to the Dallas/Fort Worth area before we come back down south and compete in Bear Creek. I'm hoping I can spend some time with Tessa this week while I'm still within driving distance. Then our relationship will have to be long distance for a while before I see her again.

If she's even willing to try to have a relationship with me.

We take the elevator downstairs and workout in the hotel gym for over an hour before we swim laps in the pool. We needed this break in between rodeos and already I'm feeling rejuvenated. Most cowboys fly or drive home when they have a week break, but because our home is so far away, we drive to the next city we compete in and stay there to prepare. The hotel costs get expensive, but we have no other choice. After our swim, we go back to our room. We rotate business calls and emails in between showering and by the time we're done, it's getting close to dinner time.

"What's for dinner? We also need to go grocery shopping to have stuff in the room," Ryan tells me after we're dressed and ready to leave.

"Alright, let me just try Tessa one more time and then we can go." I reach for my phone but Ryan grabs it before I can.

"*No!* Stop the stalker madness! You are not calling her again today! What in the hell is wrong with you? You aren't even in a relationship with this girl. You don't even know if this girl feels the same way you do. This girl might be a bat-shit crazy."

"Give me my phone, Ryan," I say calmly, silently counting to ten in my head to keep my cool before I tackle him to the ground. "You're right, I don't know who she is as a person or how she feels about me, but how else am I going to know if

I don't keep trying? Besides, aren't you interested in seeing Adeline? You couldn't even charm her enough last night to get her phone number. These American girls must see through your bullshit." With that, he hurls my phone back and fortunately, I catch it before it smashes into my face. Pointing out whenever Ryan fails with the ladies always pisses him off, especially since it doesn't happen very often.

I dial Tessa's number, expecting to hear her voice message again when I'm pleasantly surprised that the phone is picked up after the second ring. "She's not ignoring you, Rhett, she's been asleep for the last four hours," Adeline answers and I sigh in relief to actually be hearing a human voice on the other end. "Her phone was also dead from her not charging it throughout the night, so she hasn't seen or heard your voicemails and texts."

I can hear the humor in Adeline's voice and suddenly, I wish I didn't leave so many voicemails. I probably seem desperate with being so overly persistent in trying to get ahold of her. I'm not a pathetic person— I'm just determined to see her again. Time is of the essence with someone like Tessa, who has a chip as large as the state of Texas on her shoulder against men. Especially ones who are cowboys.

"I appreciate you picking up the phone and updating me. Did she have a rough night?" I ask in curiosity. Her taking a nap right now leads me to believe she didn't get a good night's sleep.

"Rough is an understatement, but she was feeling like a human after we had a late breakfast. Did you guys have a far drive to your hotel?"

"We're in Belton, which I think is a tad over an hour from you," I confirm, not knowing if she even knows where Belton is.

"Ah, yes, not too bad of a drive at all. Tell ya what, if you boys don't have plans for dinner, why don't you come to our apartment? I'll cook y'all some Tex Mex and you can spend some more time with Tessa," she offers and I can't help but pump my fist in the air with victory.

"Do you think Tessa would mind if we came over for dinner?"

I look over at Ryan, whose shakes his head in disbelief.

"Do you honestly care if she minds?" Adeline laughs, already getting a good read on me. "Here's your lesson of the day from me on Tessa. Sometimes when she's in uncertainty mode, you have to give her a big ol' shove into uncomfortable territories for her to even take the risk. She didn't tell you to go straight to hell last night, which means you've piqued her interest. But you have a big strike against you for being a cowboy. Knowing her the way I do, she wasn't going to call you back tonight. She was going to stew on it for a couple more days and probably talk herself out of it. You need face-to-face time with her and the sooner, the better. Just show up with dessert—and I mean food, not you boys as the dessert—and we'll have a great evening!"

"I owe you big time, Adeline." I get up from the sofa to put my shoes on. "What kind of dessert do you ladies like to eat?"

"Tessa loves brownies and I love butter pecan ice cream. And yes, you do owe me big time. I'll figure out payment at a later date. For now, don't dick over my friend." And with that, she hangs up on me.

"Adeline just invited us over to dinner, so here's your second chance to try not to be a prick for once and this time, get her phone number. See what being a stalker sometimes can get you?" I playfully push Ryan's shoulder so that he stumbles into the wall as we head out the door for our evening date.

## Chapter 8

### TESSA

I ROLL OVER onto my side, my brain slowly telling my body that it's time to wake up. I manage to open my eyelids and am surprised to see dusk settling in out my window. I glance at the clock and groan at the fact that it's early evening and I've slept five hours. Thank goodness I took this weekend off from working at the bar. I can't imagine going in feeling as tired as I do. I slowly rise up from my bed and go to my bathroom to take another shower, the cold water awakening my senses.

Thirty minutes later, I come out of my room to find Adeline cooking in the kitchen. She's making her world-famous fajitas with bean dip and my stomach starts rumbling at the savory smell. I walk into the kitchen to pour myself a glass of water when I stop in my tracks to look her up and down.

"Good evening, Sleeping Beauty. How are you feeling?" she asks, but I don't answer her as I notice her blonde hair is curled, she has full makeup on, and she's wearing her daisy dukes that she usually only wears when she's trying to gain some man's attention.

"Where are you going tonight?" I question while I open the fridge to get some water. I rack my brain to try to recall if she told me she was going out. Since I've been working weekends in Austin, Adeline sometimes will go out with her other friends to her favorite local country bar.

"Nowhere," she answers with a sly smile that immediately has me narrowing my eyes at her. Adeline doesn't dress like that for a night home watching Netflix.

"Really? Because you're all dolled up and are wearing shorts that barely cover your ass. I hate to hurt your feelings, but you're wasting your efforts if this was all for me. Now seriously, where are you going tonight?"

"Seriously, I'm going nowhere. Have you checked your phone yet?" She gives me another mischievous smile and I'm starting to get a little annoyed at the game she's playing.

"Ugh, stop asking me that! Why do you want me to check my phone so badly?" I walk to where my phone is charging and unplug it. When it lights up, I see I have four voicemails, all from the same phone number that is more digits than any normal North American cell phone number. The only person with an international number that would call me is Rhett, which makes my heart scream for joy that he did actually call. I click on the missed call log to find out what times he called and notice that he actually called a fifth time. Since it isn't listed as a missed call, someone— a.k.a Adeline—must have answered it.

"Why did you answer my phone the last time Rhett called?" I demand, cutting right to the chase since I know Adeline has been watching me the whole time I was looking at my phone.

"Someone needed to put that poor man out of his misery. He kept calling to see if you were okay. How sweet is that?" She perches her hip against the counter and crosses her arms under her chest, waiting for my answer.

"It's very sweet, but don't you think four times is a little too much?" According to the phone log, he called every two hours starting at 9 am. Even Adeline and I don't call each other that many times a day.

"He also sent you four texts as well. Maybe if you had responded back to him, he wouldn't have called and texted so many times." My mouth drops open in shock at her sticking up for him, plus she has been with me all day and knows exactly why I haven't responded to him.

"Let me refresh your memory since it seems the chili pepper from your cooking has given you amnesia. My phone was dead when we woke up and remained that way until we got home, where I then proceeded to go to sleep, conveniently leaving my phone out of my bedroom so that I could stay asleep. I'm sorry that my unconscious state was not efficient enough for you to not call him back right away." She laughs at my sarcasm and turns around, giving me her back while she continues cooking.

"I guess your excuses are legit. So why don't you call him back right now?" She stirs whatever she's cooking, puts the lid back on it and turns around to face me.

"Honestly, I'm not ready to talk to him." It's then that I notice she seems to be cooking enough food to feed six people. "Why is there so much food?"

"I figured you weren't ready to talk to him so I took matters into my own hands." She walks around me to put a basket of homemade tortillas on the table.

"What does that mean?" Warning bells start blaring in my head as I know I'm not going to like her answer.

"If we wait for you to take charge of your love life, we'll be old maids. Well, scratch that, you'll be an old maid because I'm not going down the man-hater rabbit hole that you're currently in. I knew you were going to talk yourself out of calling him, so I did the next best thing—I invited him and his brother over for dinner. You're welcome!" she sings out while walking back into the kitchen and pulling out four plates from the cupboard.

"You did *what*?" I screech, refusing to believe that she again involved herself in my business and invited him over without my permission. While I know Adeline has my best interests at heart,

I just don't know if I'm ready to see him again. A part of me is excited to see his ridiculously handsome face, but mentally, I don't want to get close to someone who doesn't even live in the same city, let alone the same country, as I do.

"You best be getting ready, because they'll be here any min—" The doorbell rings, cutting off Adeline's last words. "Well, look at that, they're here! I'll be kind and give you a two-minute head start back to your room so you can blow dry that hair of yours, put some makeup on, and wear something cuter than just yoga pants and a tank top. Although the tank top does show off your boobs nicely." She wiggles her eyebrows up and down while looking at my breasts. "Oh, and Tessa, don't even think of feigning ill. I'll just have him play nursemaid to you, which judging from his reaction toward you last night, he won't even hesitate in saying yes to starring in that role," she smiles wickedly at me, her eyes daring for me to disobey her.

"*I hate you!*" I hiss before running to my room to get ready. I quickly make my bed, pick up clothes from my floor and throw them in the dirty hamper in my closet. I rummage through my clothes, not satisfied with anything that I own right at this moment. I settle on a loose, black peasant top with white capri jeans. I hustle into my bathroom and am about to put on makeup when I realize that if Rhett wants to really get to know the real me, he needs to see me without any makeup on. Maybe that will change his mind about me and he'll stop calling.

*Do you really want him to stop calling you, Tessa?*

If I'm going to be honest with myself, no, I don't want him to stop calling me. But I do think this would be a good test to see if he likes au natural Tessa. I put my makeup away and braid my hair so that it's off my face. I stare at my reflection in the mirror, happy with the look that I'm going for. *We'll see if Rhett Kearney still likes what he sees after tonight.* I square my shoulders, take a deep breath and exit my bedroom.

Both men stand up when I enter and my eyes immediately drink in the tall, fine specimen that is Rhett Kearney. He's wearing a white V-neck shirt with baggy, light denim jeans and flip flops on his feet. He looks more like a professional surfer with his bronzed skin and dark blond hair than a professional bronc rider. I don't realize I am gawking at him until he's inches from me and my nose detects his scent. I almost moan out loud from how delicious he smells. The combination of his cologne with his natural body scent is something I want slathered all over my sheets so I can go to sleep with a smile on my face every night.

A quick roll around with him in my bed would take care of that need.

I gasp when he engulfs me in a tight hug, making my nipples stand to attention at the friction of being smashed into his hard chest. Before I can wrap my arms around him, he releases me and I immediately feel the loss of his body heat.

"How are you feeling today? You look beautiful." His eyes roam me up and down, making me blush at the blatant desire blazing from his gaze.

"Better, thank you. I'm sorry I missed all of your calls," I respond awkwardly, not really knowing how to address the elephant in the room.

He winks at me and turns around to grab a vase of flowers. They are beautiful lavender freesias, which are my absolute favorite flower. I look over at Adeline, who shakes her head at me, knowing that I was questioning if she told him or not.

"These are for you. I saw them and their beauty and magnificent scent reminded me of you." I stare at him in awe before taking the bouquet. I can't help myself from putting my nose into one of the flowers and sigh out loud in happiness.

"Thank you so much. Looks like you both have a knack for picking out flowers since you both chose our favorite kind." I see a bouquet of Adeline's favorite flowers—sunflowers—sitting on the kitchen counter and can only assume those are from Ryan.

*Coincidence or a sign?*

"Hope everyone's hungry because dinner is ready!" Adeline

announces and we all congregate toward the dining room table to eat. Dinner started off in awkward, nervous silence, but once Adeline asked the guys a couple of questions, conversation started to flow easier. They told us all about their family's stud farm and life back in Ireland. When I asked him what made him want to be a professional bronc rider, his response made me realize we had more things in common than I thought we had.

"I just wanted to have my own freedom to do what I wanted."

Once they were done telling us more about them, they then inquired about how Adeline and I became best friends.

"Adeline was the only one in our school who took pity on the orphaned kid from Dallas. Everyone else snubbed their noses at me because I wasn't from Bear Creek," I recall, hating those early days of middle school when I first got there.

"Orphaned?" Rhett questioned, his eyebrows raised in concern. The room gets quiet and Adeline gives me a tentative smile to continue.

"My parents were killed in a car crash when I was twelve. I was sent to live here with my aunt because she was my only living relative."

"Is your aunt still alive?" Ryan softly asks, looking at me with kindness and pity.

"Yes, she is. We don't get along very well, so as soon as I had enough money, Adeline and I moved in together and probably in the next couple of months, we're going to get a place in Austin."

"Austin? But what about the rodeo? That's a pretty long commute just to live in a bigger city." Rhett's eyes have turned into an intense green, making me wonder what he's thinking about for them to turn that way.

"Like you, I seek freedom. Being an author gives me that freedom and I can write wherever I want. With the success of my last release and the money I've saved, I can turn in my resignation after this rodeo. I can focus full-time on writing and still work part-time at the bar where I currently work weekends at. Adeline's dad has another car dealership in Austin, so it's easy for her to transfer until she gets her own business off the ground and running."

All eyes turn toward Adeline, who blushes from the attention. "I'm taking classes on graphic design at the local community college. As Tessa's assistant, I've learned that authors hire people to make their book covers, graphics and other items they need. I've already made graphics for Tessa and some other authors that she's introduced me to." She casually shrugs her shoulders, acting as if starting her own company is no big deal. "I want the same kind of freedom that we're all striving for."

"Looks like we're surrounded by some badass babes, brother," Ryan declares, looking at Adeline in appreciation.

"Let's make a toast," Rhett announces and we all raise our beer glasses. "To you ladies—may the journey to your freedom be soon and full of success, happiness, and love." Rhett stares at me while he clinks his glass to mine first before touching Ryan and Adeline's. I look down while taking a long gulp of my beer, afraid I will start choking on it if I continue staring at him. Once we are done eating, the guys help us clean up the table and kitchen, their manners showing us that their momma has taught them well.

"Come for a walk with me, Tessa," Rhett demands as soon as we finish cleaning. Before I have a chance to protest, he grabs my hand and walks us toward the door.

"Have a good time, kids!" Ryan waves at us with a cocky grin before Adeline shuts the door, her own devious smile playing on her lips. Those two seem to be made for each other with how similar they think.

Rhett adjusts our hands by intertwining our fingers together and continues leading me through the streets of my apartment complex until we reach the community pool. He lets go of my hand in order for me to type in the pool code and opens the gate for me once I get it unlocked. I stop and watch him walk toward the stairs of the pool, roll up his pant legs, slips out of his sandals and steps down onto the first step of the pool.

"Ah, feels good. Come join me." He sits down on the top stair and pats the concrete next to him. I take a shaky breath before I walk over to join him. I take off my shoes, put my feet into the water and sit down.

He's right, the pool feels amazing and not because it's that hot of an evening. The water cools down the electricity that has been buzzing between us. I can't deny the chemistry I felt between us last night and it had nothing to do with the alcohol I consumed. I feel the same desire for him tonight as I did last night. He isn't afraid to show me he feels the same way. Every time he looks at me, his eyes are storming with desire. I sneak a peek at his profile as he gazes up at the clear sky that provides us an amazing view of the stars. We sit in compatible silence, the singing of the crickets the only noise we hear. I try to think of a way to casually break our silence when he does it for me.

"I want a chance, Tessa. I want to properly date you, take you out, call you and you actually want to pick up the phone when you see it's me." I sheepishly smile at him and look at my hands so he doesn't see the embarrassment in my eyes. "I want to be part of your good days and help you handle your bad days."

*Yes!* My heart screams, ready to jump right into his arms and if it wasn't for my brain warning me to take it slow, I might have physically tackled him into the pool, begging him to stay with me forever.

"I know I need to prove myself to you, but I can't do that if you don't give me a chance." His fingers grip my chin, forcing me to look into his lust filled eyes. "You set the pace, Tessa. Just know that I'm not giving up without a chance. If you give me that chance and after a while, you still aren't interested, then I'll walk away and you never have to see me again."

His words make me frown, the thought of this not working out actually makes my heart ache. I stare into his eyes, knowing that I've got to give this man a chance otherwise it might be one of the biggest regrets in my life.

"I'll give you a chance, Rhett. Just please, don't shatter my heart," I whisper, my eyes begging him to take mercy on me because I know I'm going to fall hard for this man.

His smile is devastating and before I can recover from it, he swoops down and passionately claims my lips. He keeps his lips pressed to mine softly before sliding his hands into my hair. He parts his lips and continues massaging mine with his. So lost am I in his kiss that I don't notice when his kisses become harder, more demanding. It feels so good, so right that I crave more. I open my mouth and his tongue plunges right in, the taste of him so addicting that I sigh in contentment at finding my new favorite high.

If this is how he makes me feel from just his kisses, there will be no going back once I give him my body.

I will irrevocably be his forever.

# Chapter 9

## RHETT

LEAVING TESSA AFTER she agreed to give me a chance was physically challenging and I don't just mean because of my painful hard-on from our make-out session by the pool. I want her always by my side, especially in bed, but I know I have to take things slow with her. Feeling her reaction toward my kiss lets me know that our physical relationship is going to be off the charts, but I want it to be on her terms, when she's ready. I'm more than happy to let her navigate that aspect of our relationship because she's worth waiting for.

I asked her to lunch on Sunday since I had an inkling she wouldn't want a late night because of work on Monday, but to my surprise, she said she had to go work at the bar, saying someone called in sick so they needed her to fill in. Jealousy raced through me at the thought of other men getting to see her and for a second, I almost drove down to Austin just to sit at the bar and be with her while she worked. But I knew that wouldn't be a good idea, especially since I'm already treading on turbulent waters with her agreeing to give me a chance. So I kept myself busy by preparing for the Belton rodeo, working out and taking a nap. By the time I woke up, she was already off work so we talked during her car ride home.

Today's a new day and I'm not going to go another day without seeing her, so I decide to surprise her by driving to see her at the rodeo. Ryan, thinking my idea was genius, asked me to drop him off at Adeline's car dealership. We stopped to pick up more flowers for our women and made our way to Bear Creek. The dealership is not far from the rodeo, so I arrived within five minutes after dropping Ryan off. I'm excited to see how my lass reacts to my surprise visit, especially since I heard the disappointment in her voice when we hung up last night for her to get some sleep.

I walk around the rodeo first, admiring the state-of-the-art facility and how much money is spent on the upkeep. I make my way to the back of the arena and follow the signs to the office. I open the glass door and see an older looking gentleman talking with the receptionist. He's going over some paperwork with her, his voice deep and firm. He looks up when I walk in, his eyes sizing me up and down before plastering a smile on his face.

"Good morning, can I help you?" he asks and there's something vaguely familiar about him, which is odd to me since I've never been to Bear Creek before.

"Good morning, I'm here to see Tessa Mandel." I nod in acknowledgement to both of them. He looks at the bouquet of flowers, a sarcastic smirk playing on his lips and tells the receptionist to go get Tessa.

"I'm Tessa's boss, Caldwell George." He offers his hand for me to shake, his grip hard as if he's giving me a warning. "And who might you be?"

"Tessa's boyfriend, sir." His eyes shoot up in surprise and I take great satisfaction in saying that out loud.

"Rhett?" I hear Tessa's sweet voice and turn to watch her come down the hallway toward me. She looks so beautiful that I almost possessively growl, wanting to let everyone know she's mine. She's wearing a sleeveless blue floral sundress, her brown hair in a half up, half down style with light makeup highlighting her gorgeous face. She stops inches away from me, her eyes having that element of surprise I was hoping for.

"Tessa, this man says he's your boyfriend. As of four days ago, you didn't have a boyfriend." Her boss studies her closely, looking for answers. She casts her eyes downward and starts fidgeting with her hands. It's nice that her boss cares, but I don't like the tone of voice he's using with her.

"As of this past Saturday she does," I answer for her, enjoying how red her cheeks are getting from embarrassment.

"Tessa, is that true?" he asks incredulously and I become aware that Tessa and her boss seem to have more of a father/ daughter type of relationship. I mentally tell myself to ask her more about this when we have some privacy.

"Um, well … we're dating," she stammers out in her adorable state of flusterness.

"That's right. Exclusively. Aren't we, little lass?" I smile as she immediately nods, her reaction making me very happy that she had zero hesitations. "So if we're dating exclusively, that means I'm your boyfriend and you're my girlfriend."

She looks back and forth between her boss and the receptionist for any dispute in meaning. "Right …" she slowly says in agreement and my heart pounds in victory that I just got her to admit she's my girlfriend so quickly.

"Well, looks like congratulations are in order. What's your name, son?" He gives Tessa an intense look before his face softens.

"My name is Rhett Kearney, sir."

Mr. George blinks rapidly, a look of disbelief covering his face.

"Rhett Kearney, as in The Irish Cowboy?" Although skepticism laces his voice, I see a hint of recognition in his eyes.

"Yes, that would be the one," I confirm, enjoying watching Tessa squirm.

Mr. George looks again at Tessa in surprise and she shakes her head at him. They stare at each other, sharing something silently between them when Mr. George's demeanor completely changes.

"Well, welcome to Bear Creek Rodeo, Rhett! We're so dang excited to have you and your brother participating with us this year. Did Tessa mention that she will need you both to be here two days before the event? We want you to be a part of our press conferences and carnival that happens beforehand. Probably best you arrive on the Tuesday before the rodeo."

I look at Tessa, who glances at me with pleading eyes that beg me to agree to anything this man says. "She hasn't mentioned it yet, but you can count on us to be here early. Just send me an itinerary of dates and times and we will be there."

"Wonderful! Thank you for being so accommodating. I'll let Tessa give you the details. In fact, why don't you two go out to lunch and discuss? My treat!" He pulls out his wallet and hands Tessa a one-hundred-dollar bill that she refuses, but Caldwell George doesn't take no for an answer. She finally gives up and keeps the money.

"You two enjoy your lunch. One more thing, Mr. Kearney, that I want to make crystal clear to you." He clears his throat and leans in closer to me. "Harm Tessa in any way shape or form and I personally will make sure you never get to compete in another rodeo in this country ever again."

I immediately like this man and his loyalty to my girl. "You have nothing to worry about, sir." I match his stare with my own intensity so he sees how serious I am about her.

"We'll see about that," he replies, turns around and goes into his office.

Tessa rolls her eyes, grabs my hand, and leads us to her office. Her office is a decent size with a desk, office chair, and two other chairs across from hers. I put her flowers down on the corner of the desk and then shut her door, her eyes widening at the sound of the door locking when I twist it.

"I like your boss." I watch her back herself into a corner as I advance toward her. I can't wait any longer—I need to feel her lips on me *now*. She gasps when her back hits the wall and in one-second, I'm all over her. Her hands snake through my hair, pulling me as close as she can while my tongue thrusts inside her mouth. I grind my pelvis into her, grab both of her legs and hoist her up, forcing her to wrap her legs around me. We both moan at the same time when our cores connect with each other, the barrier of our clothes doing nothing to cool the heat between us. Her sweet, delectable mouth plays havoc on my senses and I know I need to stop this before someone knocks on her door. Her little moans of pleasure make me imagine what she'll sound like once I'm finally inside of her, the vision causing me to become so hard that I'm a mere moment away from coming all over myself.

I break away from our kiss and place my forehead against hers, our panting breaths mingling into one. We stare into each other's lust filled eyes while we try to regain our composure. Her cobalt blue eyes are shining with passion and I mentally take a photo of the way she looks, hoping I get a chance to make her look like this every day for the rest of our lives.

She gives me a quizzical look, one that I want to kiss right off her face. I sigh out loud and untangle her legs from around me, letting her slowly slide down my body. I close my eyes and grit my teeth, telling my lower half that it's time to calm down. "If we continue our exploration of each other, I will be eating *you* for lunch right here in your office. Let's go get some food in our system."

She blushes before she quickly fixes her hair, grabs her purse, and announces she's ready to go. I open the door for her and as she's about to walk past me, she leans in and whispers, "I look forward to being your meal replacement one day soon," and saunters away with a seductive smile on her on lips.

I wince as my dick tries to stand right back to attention in the confines of my jeans. Her merciless words hitting it exactly on the bullseye.

*Ah, my brazen, sexy little lass.*

With the way our bodies react to one another, that day will be coming sooner rather than later.

# Chapter 10

## TESSA

THE NEXT THREE days go by in a blur with Rhett occupying any free time I have outside of work. He consumes my every waking thought when he isn't around and when he is, he lights my body on fire with just one look. When he gives me his "I'm about to devour you" look, my body instantly reacts and I can't say no to him.

I don't want to say no to him.

Due to our busy schedules, his visits occur at nighttime with him and Ryan coming to our apartment after work. We all have dinner together, spending most of the meal getting to know each other and then playing 100 questions during dessert. I'm learning that Rhett is devilishly smart, funny and for the most part, pretty laid back. When he talks about his future, it's the same aspirations I have for myself; be my own boss and travel the world.

Once dinner is over, Rhett and I usually go for a walk, but tonight we knew we weren't going to be walking. Instead, we headed straight for his truck to continue getting to know our physical bodies, steaming up his windows with our desire for each other. What was only supposed to be a make-out session turned out to be me screaming my release from the exquisite friction against my core as I straddled and rocked against him while he devoured my lips, my breasts, and my mind. We were like teenagers making it to third base and the next step is to go all the way to home base. He just has to look at me, say my name in his husky, Irish accent and I'm his.

Rhett Kearney is a masterful thief, barreling his way into my life and stealing my heart.

I stare at him in awe while I try to come down from my orgasm. This man has made me feel so many different emotions in the short time I've known him, that I can only sum up my feelings in three ways:

Beautiful.

Fulfilling.

Terrifying.

"Come with me to Belton," he demands so softly that I blink to process what he just said to me.

"I've got to work." My heart plummets just uttering those words, but it's true. He's become the sweetest distraction, a distraction that I never wanted, but selfishly don't want to ever give up.

He smiles at me, but this time his smile doesn't reach his eyes. "You're right, I'm sorry," he says as he brings my bra straps up my arms back to my shoulders. His gentle touch sends shivers down my spine and my core muscles tighten once again with need. It dawns on me that after Belton, he will be traveling north, where he won't be able to drive so easily to see me. The thought of not seeing him for a couple of weeks makes me sick to my stomach and I start thinking of a solution.

"What about if I come up to see you perform on Saturday and spend the night?" I suggest, thinking I can work Friday and take off Saturday.

His eyes light up with happiness, making me want to always

make them light up that way. "I love that idea," he growls, grabs my neck and pulls back to him. He kisses me hard, showing just how happy he really is. I groan at the loss of his lips when he pulls away. "Lass, as much as I want to spend all night long holding you, it's getting late and we should hit the road."

I look at my watch to see that it is past 11 p.m., and he still has a long drive ahead of him. We adjust our clothing and leave the truck to go back up to the apartment. As soon as we open the door, Adeline and Ryan break apart from each other, their disheveled hair, plump lips, and rosy cheeks indicating loud and clear what we just walked in on them doing.

"Tessa, we're going to Belton!" Adeline jumps up from the couch and comes running at me.

"Wait, *we* are?" I look at Rhett, who is looking at his brother in shock.

"You asked Adeline too?" He laughs as Ryan nods and comes over to us. "That's it, Adeline, you're a keeper. Ryan is instantly smarter when he's around you."

Ryan punches him hard in the chest before throwing his arm around Adeline's shoulders. "I have a feeling this is going to be the first of many road trips together. C'mon, everyone, group hug time!"

We all laugh at him and when Rhett pulls us together for a hug, I pray that his words come true.

I WORK LATE at the bar in Austin Friday night, not getting home until around three in the morning. Rhett made me call him as soon as I got home, despite him needing sleep and having to get up early to prepare for the rodeo. Adeline let me sleep in as late as I could before waking me up to get ready to drive to Belton. We take our time getting ourselves ready, wanting to make sure we look our best since we're heading straight to the arena to meet the guys. Nervous butterflies enter my stomach as I pack my overnight bag, wondering if tonight is going to be the night that Rhett and I have sex. He said I'm in charge of that decision and while my heart is screaming yes, my brain is telling me it's too soon.

When we're packed up and ready to go, we start our journey north. While Adeline drives, I type away on my laptop, utilizing every minute I have to work on my latest book. With Rhett taking up my nights, my writing has fallen off to the side, which is exactly what I didn't want to happen. I already have my next book outlined and plotted, it's just a matter of writing it. Him being gone will be good for me since I plan on focusing all my remaining time and energy into writing. This is the book that is going to seal our fate to Austin, so I need it done before Rhett and Ryan come back to Bear Creek Rodeo to compete.

*What happens with Rhett after Bear Creek?*

The thought has me jerking up my head and inhaling sharply. My sudden movement catches Adeline's attention. "What's wrong?" she asks with concern.

"Nothing, I just thought of something," I mumble, not knowing whether or not I want to have this kind of conversation with her now. I glance at her profile and notice a certain smile on her lips, a smile that comes only when she thinks about Ryan.

"Have you considered what's going to happen when the guys aren't in Texas anymore?" I ask cautiously, trying not to sound like it's a big deal.

"Not really. I'm just trying to take it one day at a time with Ryan and not think too far ahead into the future. If I do, it will make me sad."

"Why would it make you sad?" I question, dreading to hear her answer.

"C'mon, Tessa. I know you googled Ryan when you were investigating Rhett. You've read those articles too." There were numerous articles on Ryan and his playboy status back in Ireland. Images of him with different women, none of them being a steady girlfriend.

"Maybe he's changed? Did you ever notice how long ago those articles were written?"

"The latest article was almost a year ago. It's okay, Tessa. I know I'm just a stateside fling." She tries to hide the sadness in her voice, but fails. She's starting to care for Ryan more than she wants to.

"You don't know that. Have you talked to him about it?" She looks at me as if I'm crazy before turning her attention back to the road.

"We're not like you and Rhett. You two are like magnets, glued to each other whenever you're together. Every time he leaves you, you can see it physically tortures him. Ryan isn't built that way. At this point, I just hope he will look back at me with fond memories."

Her words anger me, making me want to punch some sense into Ryan. Maybe this is all in Adeline's head though. If she hasn't talked to him about the future, then she has no idea what he's really thinking.

"If you want Ryan, then fight for him, Adeline." I punch the air, drawing a smile out of her.

"I'm not going to fight for someone who isn't interested in having an 'us'," she responds and I completely understand her meaning as that was exactly how Ty was. I was just a fling, there was no "us" to him. I was a challenge that he wanted to conquer. The thought of him puts bile in my throat. Even if Rhett and I don't work out, he's more of a man than Ty George will ever be.

I push away the negative thoughts of not having Rhett in my future and concentrate back on my writing. Before long, we are getting off the highway. Belton is larger than Bear Creek, located close to the city of Temple. The facility that houses the rodeo is a large, circular dome arena that can seat almost 7,000 people. Belton Rodeo is the closest other rodeo to Bear Creek, making it our competitor. Mr. George was happy to hear I was attending so I can be his "spy".

I text Rhett our arrival and we pick up our VIP passes and tickets at the box office. He texts me back, instructing us to go to our seats and someone will come to escort us to the dressing room. Not two minutes after we sit, a staff member comes and escorts us downstairs. The moment I see Rhett, my eyes widen and my mouth goes dry.

He's dressed in complete cowboy garb—black cowboy hat sitting low on his head, green and white checkered long sleeve shirt with his black protective vest encasing his muscular torso. His wrangler jeans are covered in brown leather chaps and black cowboy boots are on his feet. I close my parted lips for fear I might drool all over the place with how hot he looks. He approaches me slowly, his mischievous smile telling me he knows exactly what I'm thinking. He kisses me unabashedly in front of the other cowboys, leaving me hot and bothered for more.

"Your eyes are telling me you like what you see. If m'lady wishes, I would be more than willing to wear this in the bedroom for your viewing pleasure," he whispers in my ear, causing me to shiver at the mental image of him only in his hat, vest, and chaps.

"I think that needs to be arranged as soon as possible." His smile reaches his eyes, the hunger in them for me as powerful as my hunger is for him.

I pray this feeling never ends.

His lips start their descent to mine when someone interrupts us.

"Tessa, is that you?" I turn around in Rhett's arms to see the one person I never wanted to see again.

Ty George staring right back at me.

## Chapter 11

### RHETT

"GET OUT OF your head, Rhett, or you're going to screw up and get disqualified!" Ryan yells at me over the loud music. I'm sitting on my horse, getting ready for my turn to compete, but my mind is in dangerous territory.

Ty George is Tessa's ex-boyfriend.

Ty George is the man who crushed her heart.

Ty George took my girl's virginity.

As soon as he even said her name, I knew he was the asshole that crushed her heart and her reaction to him confirmed it. She was repulsed and disgusted, laced with anxiety over being in the same room with him. Jealousy boiled through me, my hands fisted at my side, itching to smash through his face. Punching him would disqualify me from the competition, hurting my rank in the standings to get to Nationals. I'm sitting pretty right now in the top ten and with the last remaining rodeos left, I can't afford any mistakes.

Or distractions.

I first met Ty when we were both on the Australian Pro

Rodeo circuit. He was a slimy bastard then and it looks like things haven't changed. He's a gifted saddle bronc rider whose narcissistic ways will ruin his career.

I, personally, am looking forward to when that day arrives.

"Beat him on the scoreboard, Rhett, not with your fists. Get into the game!" Ryan slaps my back before moving over onto the opposite rail to watch and cheer me on. I take a couple of breaths and nod at him, acknowledging that I heard him loud and clear.

*Beat him on the scoreboard.*

I hear the announcer tell the crowd to get ready, the bucking chute gate opens and we're off. I focus on my legs, positioning them properly at the horse's shoulders until I feel the horse's feet hit the ground and then I start moving. The crowd fades away and it's just me and the horse. I work at maintaining my upper body balance while moving my legs in sync with the bucking motion of the horse. I zero in on its rhythm and for eight-seconds, I ride it as if we were one.

Those eight-seconds feel like eternity.

When the buzzard sounds, the pickup men ride up next to me, helping calm the horse down. As soon as it's safe, I immediately jump off and run in the opposite direction from where they take the horse. I wave to the crowd and pump my first at Ryan before scanning the crowd for Tessa. I see her jumping up and down in excitement with Adeline, clapping and cheering with everyone else.

I've dreamt of this moment, having her with me at all times, cheering me on. In my dreams, I was filled with pride and lust.

Right now I look at her and only see Ty George's grimy fingers all over her.

I turn in the opposite direction and stalk back to Ryan, the dark cloud that has my mood violently churning into a tornado.

"You just killed it out there and you're still thinking about him? Let it go, Rhett! She's here with *you*, not him!" Ryan shakes his head in disgust at me and stops walking beside me. "Take a shower and cool down. Don't throw away all of your hard work for a worthless, piece of shit like him." He walks back toward the chute while I head to the locker room to try to wash my foul mood off me before I say and do something stupid.

RYAN AND I both placed first in our respective categories. I was somewhat content beating Ty on the scoreboard, but the full satisfaction came when Tessa rushed into my arms in the dressing room and openly kissed me in front of him, making sure he witnessed not only her kiss, but her hand staking its claim on my ass. Possessive Tessa makes me want to throw her over my shoulder and claim her in the janitor's closet right now.

Her actions make it loud and clear—she's mine.

But Ty is a calculated guy, one who always has to have the last parting shot. When he saw we were close to crossing the threshold of the door to leave, he dealt one quick last jab for everyone to hear.

"Hope you enjoy my leftovers, Kearney."

My vision went red and it took Ryan and four other guys to hold me back from destroying him. I was within a couple of centimeters from his face, wanting to pummel him into the ground for talking about her like that. For even being in the same room as her.

It was Tessa's voice that finally got me to calm down and remember that I can't physically hurt him. I can only physically hurt his rank and money earnings by beating him at Finals.

We go to dinner afterwards, but I don't have much of an appetite with his words playing on repeat in my head. My mood has affected everyone and this becomes the quietest meal we have ever had together. I catch Tessa and Adeline glancing at each other often, silent messages being communicated between them with their eyes. What should've been a celebratory evening has turned into one I would like to forget.

"Rhett, I need you to buy me a beer *now*," Ryan demands as he stands up and comes next to my chair. I give him a questioning look because our waitress is more than capable of getting the beer for him. The look in his eyes is screaming for me to accompany him to the bar to talk. I reluctantly get up and excuse myself from the ladies.

"You're losing her, brother. You're making her feel that tonight was all her fault."

"How would tonight be all her fault?" I question, not understanding his logic.

"You're barely talking to her since you let that asshole into your head. It's obvious she's feeling you don't want her anymore because of her past with him. Look at her—don't you see that they're talking about bolting right now?"

I look over at the table to see Adeline adamantly talking to Tessa, who's nodding, her beautiful face painted in sadness.

"Of course I still want her! I'm just having a hard time forgetting that she's been with him."

"Why does that matter to you? That's in the past! She could be doing a million other things right now, but she chose to be here with you!" Ryan throws up his hands in exasperation.

"But he's the reason why she won't give her heart to me. Him! Out of all the men in this world, that bastard is the reason!" I shake my head in disbelief, not understanding how he couldn't see how lucky he was. Yes, it's my gain, but it comes at a price.

Her hatred for cowboys.

Her fear of getting hurt again.

"You need to take him out of the equation, Rhett. Haven't you noticed that you're winning her heart? *You!* No one else but you!"

"I know, but what happens when I'm gone these next couple of weeks? What happens if she decides I'm not worth the risk of getting hurt again?" I ask, letting my real fear be known to him. Seeing Ty again might make her remember that pain he inflicted on her and I won't physically be here to change her mind.

Ryan places his hand on my shoulder and squeezes. "That's the risk that you're going to have to take. If she can't see what a better man you are, then maybe she isn't the one for you." He looks me dead in the eyes when saying that and I know he's right.

I shake my head and start to chuckle, not believing the words that are coming out of his mouth right now.

"What's so funny? Have you gone mad?" he asks, a smile starting to form on his lips at seeing me laugh.

"No, I just can't believe that out of all the people in this world, you're the one giving me advice on my love life." If my sister could hear our brother now, she would declare that Ryan is the one who's gone mad. Truth be told, I think Adeline is opening up my brother's eyes on the kind of love he can have with her.

"I can't believe the shit that is coming out of my own mouth either. Who *am* I right now?" he jokes, pulling me in for a quick hug.

"Thanks for talking some sense into me, brother," I say with sincerity. We walk back to our table to join our girls.

"Ladies, I apologize for being a grouchy jerk tonight." I sit down next to Tessa and turn to look at her, grabbing her hand to gain her attention. "I'm sorry I embarrassed you in the dressing room. I couldn't control my reaction as I won't stand for anyone talking about you that way." I place my hand against her cheek and gently caress it before I bring my lips to hers for a quick, gentle kiss. She exhales a shaky breath when we're done and smiles, her eyes watery from unshed tears. I hate that I'm the cause of them and silently vow to never make her feel that way again.

"His words are worthless, just like he is. We can't let him affect us." I nod, wanting her to see that I'm listening and I will try for her sake.

"I don't even like rodeos, but you were magnificent tonight. I couldn't take my eyes off you. I'm so proud of you," she whispers as she squeezes my hand back. "Thank you for inviting me to be here with you tonight."

Her words knock the breath right out of me, the need and want I have for her pumping my heart so fast that it feels it might explode out of my chest.

I've fallen hard and fast for Tessa Mandel and I don't want to waste anymore time not proving it to her.

"Ryan," I say in a low, commanding voice while my eyes still hold Tessa's gaze captive. "Tessa and I are leaving now." I don't even ask Tessa if she's ready to go. The need to physically devour every inch of that creamy, silky body of hers is a hunger that I must satisfy now. The flare of desire that sparks in her eyes tells me she's ready and willing.

"You two go do all the things that I would do, please." He winks at me while Tessa gives Adeline a hug goodbye. I grab Tessa's hand and we walk briskly out of the restaurant. Thankfully the restaurant is in walking distance from the hotel and Ryan and I got separate rooms knowing the girls were coming up this weekend. We walk in silence, no words needed to fill the time as the anticipation of what's to come buzzes between us.

I unlock the door to the hotel room and hold it open for her. I watch her walk all the way to the bed and once she hears the click of the door, she turns around and stares at me. I stand there and search her eyes, waiting for the sign from her on my next move. We gaze at each other, the air starting to feel heavy with yearning. Seconds seem to feel like minutes until she makes the first move. In one swift motion, she pulls her sundress off, standing there in only her cowgirl boots and matching bra and panties.

Hot pink and black lace accentuate all the right curves of her body, but I prefer her lingerie to be elsewhere.

On the floor where it belongs.

I stalk toward her, my chest rising and falling hard with every step I take until I crush her against me, my mouth staking its claim. While my tongue invades her luscious mouth, our hands work quickly to get rid of the remaining barriers between us. Digging into my pocket, I withdraw a small foil packet for protection before discarding my jeans to the floor. I gently lay her down on the bed, my eyes drinking in the beauty of her nakedness. She watches me admire her and then she glances downward, her eyes widening when she sees how hard I am for her. When she looks back up at me, it isn't fear that I see in her. It's hunger.

I lay my body over hers, our mouths opening up in frenzied greed to taste each other. She opens her legs wider for me to settle between, but I know if I come anywhere near her core, I won't last very long. To distract myself, I break our kiss and my mouth starts its slow assault down her neck, trailing wet, hot kisses all the way down to her breast where I flick my tongue over the bud of her nipple.

"Please," she begs, her hands roaming over my back down to my ass where she cups my cheeks to try to guide me into her. It takes every ounce of willpower not to obey. I want to hear her say exactly what she wants from me. I want to hear those words come out of her savory mouth.

"Please what, lass? Tell me what you want. You know what I want? I want to slide right into your warmth and stay there until I make you forget your own name." She moans loudly at my words, her teeth grazing my earlobe shooting sparks down my spine. My hand lightly massages down her body, traveling south to feel if she's ready for me. My fingertip rubs against her bud, causing her hips to move against me. Her moaning gets louder, the sensual sound making me ache with the pain of needing to be inside her.

"Now," she stammers, her voice raspy with longing. "I need you now, Rhett!"

I smile down at her as I put the condom on, position myself at her opening and slowly slide inside of her. Sweat forms on my forehead as I try to restrain myself from not plunging fully inside of her. She's so tight and slick, but made perfectly for me. I slowly inch myself fully into her and as soon as I start to feel her walls tightening around me, I start thrusting. I slowly increase my rhythm, watching wave after wave of pleasure play on her face. When her eyes flash open and she starts panting, I know she's on the verge of ecstasy. She grabs hold of my ass and the friction with the increased tempo sends her over the edge.

Watching her climax is all I need to find my own release. As I feel my body explode inside of her, I realize this is what a piece of heaven must feel like as I've never felt this overwhelming feeling of love for another person. My heart is beating for her, for us.

I don't have time to think of the consequences of my actions before I look into her eyes, the eyes I want to stare in forever before I whisper what my heart is screaming in my chest.

"I love you, Tessa."

## Chapter 12

### TESSA

FOUR WEEKS WENT by until I got to see Rhett again after our night together. A night where he took my body to places it had never been before. A night where there was a shift in our relationship. A night where he uttered those three little words.

Every girl wants to have the man of their dreams say they love them. And here I had that man, yet I was terrified of those words. I was physically unable to say it back to him, emotionally blocked because everyone I have loved had been taken from me or left me.

At first, I didn't think much about it, chalking it up to the fact that maybe he's confusing lust for love, but he kept telling me he loved me after every conversation we had when he was away.

*Is he crazy for loving me so quickly or am I crazy for questioning why?*

"I don't know how that man puts up with you," Adeline said when I asked her opinion on it.

"You believe you can fall in love with someone within a month?" I asked, skepticism lacing my voice with the fact that she could actually think so.

"Yes, I do. It has to be the most intensive, all-consuming, overwhelming feeling every time you are with that person. You can't imagine life without them. You can't go without a day or couple of hours without talking to them. You don't want to ever be without them. Do you feel that way about Rhett?"

*Yes!*

"I don't know," I responded instead, scared to even recognize that I could feel that way about someone so soon.

Adeline rolled her eyes, not believing me for one-second. "Don't bullshit yourself, Tessa. Stop being so scared and live! Do you miss Rhett?"

"Yes."

"Do you trust Rhett?"

"Yes."

"Does the thought of him with another woman make you physically ill?"

"It makes me more physically violent, like I want to punch someone." I've never gotten into an altercation with another woman before, but if anyone puts their hands on Rhett in front of me, I might go crazy.

"Then you are in love with him. Don't play games with him. You've been worried this whole time that he would hurt you, yet you're the one holding the strings to his heart."

Her words resonated with me, especially when I would see the disappointment in Rhett's eyes during our video chats after I wouldn't say the words back. I tried to talk with him about it one night during our phone conversations, but instead he cut me off, saying he understood and that he knows when I do say it, it will be because I meant it and didn't feel forced. I made sure my actions made up for my lack of words as best as I could while he was gone. I sent him constant texts of encouragement, sexy photos, and told him every day how much I missed him.

I knew I had to make the most of my time while he was away because once he came back for the rodeo, I wanted to spend every minute I could with him. Any free moment I had, I was writing. I managed to finish my novel after the second week of his absence and published it one week later. Three days before he was expected back, it hit the *USA Today Bestseller's List.*

The following day, I turned in my resignation.

At first, Mr. George refused it. "Are you telling me you're quitting because my son's competing here next weekend? I won't accept that from you, Tessa!"

"I would never give him that satisfaction," I said in amusement at Mr. George's response. "No offense, sir."

"None taken. I know my son is a jackass," he said in frustration, causing me to laugh out loud. "Why are you leaving me, Tessa? Is it because of Rhett Kearney?"

"No, sir, it has nothing to do with him. You see, I've had a dream for myself and I worked hard enough that it came to fruition." I revealed everything to him and once I was done, he sat back and stared at me, emotionless. When the silence became uncomfortable, that's when he finally spoke.

"I didn't know your momma and daddy, but I have no doubt they're smiling down on you from heaven, incredibly proud of the legacy they left behind." I hadn't cried in a long time over my parents, but his words made me tear up.

"What's going to happen with you and Rhett?" he asked after we decided what my last day at work would be.

"Who knows," I responded with a shrug. "I'm going to enjoy every moment I have with him and we'll see where it goes."

The anticipation of seeing Rhett again was almost unbearable with the last week being torturous. My body was buzzing with the need to be able to touch him again. When the boys arrived back in town, Ryan and Adeline stayed in the hotel the guys had while Rhett moved in with me for the week of the rodeo. I loved waking up in his arms, coming home to him after work and having him completely overwhelm my body in bed. I could get used to this kind of life with Rhett, but we haven't even discussed our future plans. He'll be staying with me for one more week after the rodeo, but then Ryan and him plan on heading back to Ireland for their month-long break before Nationals.

I refused to worry about the future and the unknown status of our relationship. Instead, I'm focused on us in the present and every moment I have with him.

SATURDAY HAS ARRIVED and my last rodeo at Bear Creek is about to start. There's a spring in my step and I can't stop smiling. With Bear Creek being a small town, word spread like wildfire about my resignation. Most people who work at the rodeo are lifers, so they were quite surprised with the news, especially not knowing the real reason. I asked Mr. George to keep my author identity quiet and he did, telling people I had a "job" lined up in Austin.

He wasn't exactly lying.

Most of the part-time contractors who I only see during rodeo week have come and wished me farewell. It has been a busy day, with showtime in less than two hours. Rhett and Ryan should be arriving soon and I can't wait to watch my man take first place.

I walk around the arena and sit down in one of the seats, watching the grounds crew get the pit ready. It dawns on me that while I'm eternally grateful to Mr. George for giving me my first full-time job, I will not miss this place. It was a stepping-stone to help me get to where I wanted to go in my life and I will look back at it with fond memories. Even though I experienced heartache from Ty, I came out a stronger person because of it.

My phone vibrates in my pocket, alerting me to a text message. I pull it out to see Mr. George needs my help back in the office. I take one last look around before heading there. When I arrive, Mr. George is nowhere to be found, but a huge bouquet of freesias and lilies are on my desk with a note from Rhett.

*Onto bigger and better things, Little Lass.*

*Congratulations on your last rodeo!*

*I love you,*

***Rhett***

Tears start to pool in my eyes at his sweet words and thoughtful gesture. Today is supposed to be his big day with this being the last rodeo before Nationals. He should be mentally preparing himself for tonight, not thinking about me and how this is my last rodeo. But that's the thing about Rhett; he's selfless and always concerned about me and my happiness.

*How did I get so lucky?*

I send him a quick text thanking him before I hear Mr. George call my name. I put my phone back in my pocket and go help him.

Three hours later and I'm still running around like a crazy woman, helping out anyone who seems to be having a problem. I get a text from Adeline alerting me that Rhett will be up soon. I manage to make it to my seat just as Ty finishes. Ty and Rhett are neck and neck in the standings as of today, but that will change again once all scores are tallied.

Ty waves to the crowd, the cheers for the hometown cowboy deafening. I refuse to clap for him and am disappointed when I see he scored an 86.

"That's pretty good," I tell Adeline, my nerves giving me anxiety. Fortunately, Rhett is the last rider for his competition so he knows he needs to beat Ty's score. I say a little silent prayer to keep Rhett safe because although I want him to beat Ty, his safety is much more important to me.

I see Rhett and his horse in the chute. As the announcer tells the crowd to get ready, I take a deep breath and hold it for those eight-seconds he manages to stay on his horse. Not only does he stay on, but he does it flawlessly, looking like he's in total synchronization with the horse.

I jump out of my seat as soon as that bell indicates the end of his ride. The pickup men flank each of his sides and he gets off. He waves at the crowd, but I see his eyes searching ... searching for me. When he finally sees me, he points at me and blows me a kiss.

I love that he searches for me in the crowd, needing to see me.

I love that he just publicly blew me a kiss.

I love his determination and grit to be the best.

I love ... *him.*

I love Rhett Kearney.

"Adeline," I grab her arm in excitement and start shaking it. "I love him, Adeline! *I love him!*"

"I've already told you that you do! Now go down there and tell him!"

"What, now?" My eyes bug out of my head at her suggestion.

She gives me an exasperated look and starts pushing me toward the exit. "Yes, now! He needs to finally hear it and what better place than here?"

I don't think anymore, I just go. I run to the door that leads me downstairs to the dressing room. I race down the stairs and pull open the door, only to stop short. The hallway is full of people, cowboy hats everywhere. I make my way through the crowd, my heart pounding so loudly in my ears that I don't hear anything else. I get closer to the dressing room when I see him outside of the door, being interviewed by a television crew. I stare at him, marveling at how damn sexy he is and that he's all mine. As if he feels he's being watched, his eyes meet mine and he smiles that special smile that is only for me.

As he finishes up his interview and locks his eyes back with mine, it's like time freezes. Everyone and everything fades away and it's just the two of us. I sprint toward him and fling myself into his arms. Our lips crush against one another in a mind-numbing kiss.

"Hey cowboy," I pant out, trying to regain my composure, breathless from his lips on mine.

"Kiss all the cowboys that way do ya, little lass?" he teases, melting me with a wicked smile.

"Nope." I shake my head since he knows that he's the exception to my "no cowboy" rule. Placing my hands against his cheeks, I make sure he's looking me straight in the eyes so he can see how serious I am. "Only the ones I love."

His eyes widen and his grip on me tightens. He's about to kiss me again when we hear his name being called out.

"Rhett, Rhett!" Ryan yells as he runs down the hallway. "You scored a 90! We're going to Las Vegas!" Ryan throws his arms around both of us as we celebrate his victory. "I'm going to call our parents," he offers and leaves to find a quiet place to make the call.

"You know you're coming with me to Ireland, right?" he tells me with a wicked grin. I nod, excitement racing through me at the idea of going to Ireland with him. My smile fades and I look into his eyes, needing to tell him the words he's been waiting to hear.

"I love you, Rhett. You have me, body and soul," I say before kissing him with all the passion I can exude. He breaks our kiss, resting his forehead against mine while staring intently into my eyes.

"Forever, Tessa?"

"Forever."

*We're not done yet... are you ready for Ryan and Adeline's love story?*
*Turn the page!*

# *The Celtic*
# COWBOY

## JESSICA MARIN

# Chapter 1

## Ryan

THE VASTNESS OF the Atlantic Ocean surrounds us while cruising at 39,000 feet on this clear, sunny day. The humming of the jet engines has lulled most passengers to sleep, yet I stare out of the window, hypnotized at the beauty of the sapphire colored water. I'm too excited to sleep — the anticipation of landing in America buzzing through my body, making my leg bounce with nervous energy. I've been dreaming about this very moment — coming to the States to compete in their Pro Rodeo Cowboy Circuit. Becoming the best bull rider in the world has always been the goal and I'm one step closer to making it my reality. The best part about all of this is that I'm not alone on my journey. My brother, Rhett, is also making his debut in the American Pro Rodeo Circuit, trying to win the title of the best saddle bronc rider in the world.

Rhett and I knew we wanted to be professional cowboys ever since we were young lads. Our family owns one of the premier stud farms in all of Ireland and our father used to take us with him when he would deliver horses to his clients in Spain. It was there that we experienced our first rodeo. Rhett has always been drawn to horses, but for me, there was something exhilarating about trying to ride a fifteen-hundred-pound animal for eight-seconds without being crushed to death. Our parents weren't too keen on the idea of both of their sons riding on top of bucking mammals and thought we would outgrow our new obsession.

To their chagrin, we became even more passionate about it.

There isn't much rodeo action in Ireland, so once we graduated school, we both headed to other countries. I stayed close to home and started my career in Spain while Rhett traveled all the way to Australia. He asked me to go with him, but being so far away from home just didn't appeal to me, which is quite shocking since I'm usually the rebellious one. Rhett, on the other hand, couldn't wait to get out of Ireland. Rhett is five years older than me and has always been curious about what was beyond our homeland. I've never had that desire. I liked being close to my family and working on the farm in the off-season. Once Rhett went to Australia, we barely saw him. During his off seasons, he would stay there and only came home on holidays. We would talk weekly on the phone, making plans to fulfill our dreams of going to America one day.

But both of our careers had to be put on hold when our father was thrown off a horse and shattered his leg. Rhett and I came home to help our sister and mother run the farm. Even though having Rhett home helped enormously, he was unhappy. His carefree, joking attitude left and was replaced with a moody, more serious version of himself. Even though he has not publicly come right out and said it, Rhett doesn't want to inherit the farm. As the eldest, he's expected to take it over once our parents retire, but that just isn't in his blood. With father's injury, I think Rhett thought his rodeo days were numbered. I hated seeing this side of my brother and once I saw our father was going to be just fine, I told him it was our time to go to America. It took some convincing and as I look over at him, a frown on his face as he watches a movie, I still think he feels guilty for leaving.

His frown only accentuates his good looks. His skin is tan from working outside, his dark blond hair messy from his hands combing through it. His emerald green eyes focus on the scene in the movie. He never once acknowledged the stares and smiles ladies were giving him as they walked past us toward their seats. I, on the other hand, took account all the women that noticed me and smiled right back at them. One of the flight attendants has been very accommodating, stopping by our seats on numerous occasions to see if we needed anything. I finally put her to work, ordering myself a beer, making sure she saw my appreciation of her curvaceous body. Her mouth curved into a knowing smile, her eyes raking down my own body before she left. I shift in my seat, the tightening of my groin making me uncomfortable as I think of all the things I can do with that luscious body of hers. Before long she's walking back with my drink. She purposely sticks her breasts close to my face as she lowers herself to place the drink on the tray. Along with the beer, she leaves a folded piece of paper. I give her a questioning smile before she nods at me and heads to the back. I open the note, my eyebrows shooting up in surprise at what it says.

Meet me in the back gallery bathroom in five minutes.

I've never joined the Mile High Club before and I'm not opposed to popping my cherry on this flight. I wonder if she picks up men like this often — not that I care, since I'm ready and willing to join her. I smile and am about to fold the note when Rhett's hand shoots out and grabs it from me.

"You better not be considering this," he warns, his eyes storming in annoyance as he balls the note in his fist.

"Are you daft? Of course I'm considering it! What hot blooded male wouldn't?" I burst out loudly. I smile in apology at the lady with her child across the aisle from me and turn back to Rhett. "Why would I deprive myself of a good time with a hot flight attendant?"

"Because you need to think of your reputation, that's why. Plus, you don't know where that girl's been. Don't you wonder if she takes strange men back there all the time?"

I refuse to tell him that the thought did cross my mind and it still wasn't going to deter me.

"Maybe I'm the best-looking bloke whose shown interest in her and she wants to take advantage of it," I say, trying to justify her reasoning for having sex with a complete stranger in the middle of a flight, when really, my argument is weak.

"Don't be a conceited asshole. She gets plenty of men hitting on her. You've already slept with all of Kildare and half of Dublin, I don't need you sleeping with all of America too."

"I haven't slept with that many women," I grumble, not wanting to discuss my extracurricular activities with my brother, who frowns upon them. I can't help that I gravitate toward the female population, nor can I help that they enjoy my company as well. With billions of women on this Earth, why should I just be settling with one? I'm young and have no desire to settle down right now. Rhett wants to meet "The One" and find a partner that he can go on adventures with.

I don't even think I believe that there is one woman for me.

"Let's lay some ground rules right now for this trip. Number one — no sleeping with complete strangers who we meet on airplanes. Number two — no sleeping with any women associated with the rodeos we are competing in. Number three — no sleeping with anyone on this trip *period*!" Rhett looks intensely at me so that I know he means business. Number three is so ridiculous that I can't help but burst out laughing at the audacity of it.

"You can't be serious!" I laugh, waiting for the punchline of his joke. When he continues to stare at me, I realize he's not joking. "There's no way that's not happening. We are in America for close to a year! You're really asking me to be celibate the whole time?"

"Not unless you get a serious girlfriend," he answers, a smirk playing on his lips since he knows that won't be happening.

"You know that isn't going to happen with the schedule we mapped out. We're in and out of most cities within forty-eight hours."

"Look at it as another challenge, brother. If you want to be the best bull rider in the world, you need to focus on staying healthy, getting enough rest, and training."

"Having sex *is* training! It helps with my stamina on staying on top of that bull for eight-seconds." I try to reason with Rhett, who isn't buying any of my bullshit.

"If we want a shot at Nationals, we need to stay focused. No girls as distractions, you hear me?"

"Five hours into this trip and I'm already regretting being here with you," I respond back, not in the least bit joking either. I have no problems leaving Rhett at the airport and us going our separate ways if this is how he's going to act for nine months. I've worked too hard not to have some fun along the way. Rhett might have to remain celibate in order to perform better, but I sure as hell don't.

"I bet one American lass bats their pretty little eyelashes at you and you're a goner," I tease, knowing that Rhett's picky when it pertains to the women he decides to spend his time with. "Did you forget how handsome you are? These lasses have no chance once they see you. Even worse when they see me." I nudge his shoulder with my own, finally getting a smile out of him.

"All I ask is that you behave, Ryan. Please try to stick to the rules," he demands before sticking his headphones back into his ears to listen to the movie.

I lean back into my seat and close my eyes. There's no way I plan on abiding to any of Rhett's rules, yet I really don't want to travel the country by myself. America is much bigger than Ireland and Spain and since Rhett and our sister made most of our travel plans, it would be pretty stupid of me to ditch him just because I want to get laid. A headache starts to form and I sigh while I push my seat back in order to try to relax.

*This is going to be a long nine months.*

# Chapter 2

## Adeline

I LOOK AROUND the office to see if anyone is watching me. It's quiet right now, with most of the salespeople on the floor working with customers. I just finished updating the car inventory report for my father, making my to-do list complete. With him and no-one else in sight, I reach down into my tote bag and grab my laptop. I quickly open up Illustrator and continue to work on the graphic I'm creating for the new book my best friend is releasing this week. I unlock the word document she sent me with some teasers from her book, copy one, and paste it onto the photo of the half-naked man. I play around with the format, insert some creative fonts and lean back to assess my work. I smile slowly, proud of how far I've come in just a short amount of time with my side career as a graphic designer. Well, calling myself a graphic designer might be a stretch since I only design for Tessa, my best friend, and one other author she has introduced me to. Still, I'm getting pretty damn good as this teaser I just made for her is very sexy—exactly what she wanted it to be.

"Adeline, I need you to pick up your brother for me today." My father's voice startles me and I slap my laptop shut, but not before he sees what I was doing.

"How many times have I told you not to create that smut while working here?" My father isn't a fan of the type of novels Tessa writes, nor is he happy that I help her. He thinks her "Yankee" ways are changing my behavior, despite him knowing that Tessa isn't even a Yankee.

She's from Dallas.

But since that's "up north" to him and more progressive than Bear Creek, he's convinced that she's a bad influence on me, even though both my mother and I tell him he's being archaic.

"I'm sorry, Daddy, I won't do it again," I lie, batting my eyelashes at him because we both know I *will* do it again. There's just no point in arguing with him over it. I've been working at my father's car dealership now for six years, ever since I graduated from high school. I started off first as a part-time receptionist while I went to community college. I've moved my way up to his assistant when his former one resigned two years ago. It's a steady job with good pay and I'm grateful to my father for the opportunity, but it isn't what I want to do with the rest of my life.

Being my own boss and getting *out* of Bear Creek is exactly what I want to do with my life.

People who are born in Bear Creek are usually lifers and with my family being town royalty, my dreams would be considered blasphemy. I'm the daughter of one of the most famous football players ever to come out of Bear Creek. Clint Murphy has been a celebrity since he was in high school, becoming the first quarterback from Bear Creek High to play in the NFL for fourteen seasons, managing to play all of those seasons with one team. He was forced into retirement early due to numerous concussions. Once retired, my father used his fame to obtain partners and invest in numerous businesses, with majority of them being car dealerships around southeast Texas. He also invested a lot into the Bear Creek community, making him a household name around town. While his generosity for the community comes from a genuine place in his heart, he and my mother enjoy the perks of being local celebrities. What they failed to think about was how it would affect their children in both a negative and positive way.

My brothers, Colt and Carson, are following exactly in my father's footsteps. Colt is the starting quarterback at the University of Texas and Carson is in his junior year at Bear Creek High, while being one of their best wide receivers. Both of them are big men on their respective campuses, relishing in being popular, adored and loved. My parents' life revolves around football schedules, making sure nothing stands in their way from being at every single one of their home and away games.

"Why do I have to pick Carson up when he has his own car?" I question, not understanding my father's request to go get him from practice. My father gifted all of us with brand new cars when we got our licenses. I don't think I've seen my mother as happy as she is now that she's no longer anyone's chauffeur.

"Your brother got his car taken away from him for making some poor choices at school."

"What did he do?" I sigh, knowing it must have been pretty bad for our dad to take away his truck. Colt and Carson could get away with murder and my father would turn a blind eye as long as it didn't affect them playing in any games.

"He was caught taking a shower in the girl's locker room … with the star volleyball player."

I can't help the giggle that escapes me at his look of disgust. Some dads would have been proud of their son for getting action, but not ours. He knows both of my brothers might have the chance at a long career in the NFL, so he tries to keep them on the straight and narrow path. Seems like he's losing that battle when it comes to Carson, who's known to have his own little harem at school.

"The Coach and I managed to persuade the principal not

to suspend him since we're one game away from making the playoffs. He needs to be focusing all of his energy on football, not silly little girls."

"I'm sure her parents don't think she's a 'silly little girl,' Daddy." I shake my head at how disrespectful he is toward the girl who I'm sure Carson persuaded to take a shower with him. "Why can't Mom pick him up?"

"Your mother has a late hair appointment and refused to reschedule it."

"One of his many minions can't drop him off?" I keep asking, not really wanting to go get my brother. Tessa and I have our own apartment together and we planned to order in Chinese food and work on the last pieces we need for her release day. No matter if this release is a big hit or not, we're going to celebrate in Austin this weekend by treating ourselves to a nice dinner and one night in a hotel.

"Why don't you want to go get him? Do you have a date tonight?" he asks, his eyes getting wide with hope.

"No, why?" I scrunch up my nose at the yucky thought and look at him suspiciously.

"Then you have nothing better to do than to go spend some time with your baby brother. It's bad enough you won't come to his or Colt's away games. We barely see you anymore and your mother and I don't like it." He takes his wallet out of his pocket, grabs a one-hundred-dollar bill, and dangles it in front of me. "Go get your brother, grab some BBQ and bring it home so we can have a family dinner together." His eyes are demanding, testing to see if I defy his orders, but he knows I won't. With a heavy sigh, I take the money and stuff it into my purse.

"What time do I have to go get him?" I reluctantly ask, not really looking forward to another family dinner where the topic of conversation is all about football and why I'm not married yet.

My father glances at his watch and grimaces. "Right about now. I'll see you at home in an hour." He pats me awkwardly on the shoulder and walks away. I send a quick text message to Tessa telling her the change in plans, stuff my laptop in my bag, grab my car keys and head out the door.

Fortunately the drive to Bear Creek High takes only ten minutes and my brother is already showered and dressed, waiting outside with a group of guys. His whole demeanor changes once he sees that it's me picking him up. His smile turns into a frown, his shoulders sink, and I can see him groaning as everyone escorts him up to my car to say hello. I can't help that all these boys think with their brains below their belts and hit on me every chance they get. If it was up to me, I would never come to any of my brother's football games, but there would be a good possibility that I'd be disowned.

"Well, aren't you a sight for sore eyes, Miss Adeline," his assistant coach drawls out as he opens the door for Carson to get in. He stares at my face before his eyes wander lecherously up and down my body, making me feel like I need to take another shower from his grossness. I receive the evil eye from Carson while he gets into the car, warning me to be nice to his coach. Andrew Knox has been an assistant coach at Bear Creek for four years now and while most women would think he's cute and a catch since he's one of the younger coaches on staff, he's always given off a creepy vibe to me. Plus, he's my brother's coach. I wouldn't date anyone who has any association with my brothers.

"Good evening, Coach Knox," I politely comment with a nod. "Hope practice was successful tonight."

"Oh it was. Your brother worked hard getting ready to play Beaumont this weekend. You coming to the game?" I take a peek at my brother's face out of my peripheral vision and can tell he's uncomfortable, knowing full well what his coach is up to. Andrew Knox doesn't do small talk, especially with a female.

"No, I can't this Friday. I already have plans." My brother looks my way, relief shining bright in his eyes. Carson doesn't care if I don't come to his away games, but it looks like he's especially grateful that I'm not coming to this one.

"That's a shame. I was hoping you would finally take me up on my offer of dinner after what I know will be a victory." He smiles at me and I can't help but to throw up a little in my mouth.

"Since hell hasn't frozen over yet, it looks like you'll be waiting for a long time. I suggest you take someone who's receptive to the idea of sharing a meal with you. I do thank you for the offer though." My voice oozes out sweetness, but my eyes are as serious as a car accident. The smile on his face falters, the collective gasps of his players behind him fill the night air. My brother groans and covers his face with his hands in mortification.

Andrew's eyes turn cold and he slams my car door shut before leaning inside the open window frame for one last word. "No wonder you're still single, Miss Murphy. No man would ever want to put up with a mouth like that."

"Their loss if they don't like a little spice in their life," I answer with a bright smile and give him a wink. "Toodles boys!" I put the car into drive and press hard on the gas, my tires skidding out as we accelerate ahead. I look in the rearview mirror to see all of them still staring at us.

"Why? Why did you have to do that to me, Adeline?" Carson whines from behind his hands. "Everyone is going to be talking about this tomorrow at school."

"Did you really want me to go to dinner with him? He's a skeezeball, Carson! I have more respect for myself than that!"

"Couldn't you just accept to go on one date with him and then turn him down nicely afterwards?"

"*No!*" I look at him incredulously, not believing what I'm hearing. "First off, he's your coach! Do you know how many more rumors would start if I did go out on one date with him? Secondly, he's a douchebag! I don't date men like that."

"No one would hit on you if you had a boyfriend they all knew about. Why aren't you dating anyone right now? Is it because you prefer women over men?" At first I think he's joking, but then my mouth drops open in shock when I see the seriousness in his eyes.

"Seriously, Carson?" My voice goes up an octave, my frustration with my brother's ignorance at an all-time high. "What do you think?"

"I don't think you do, but Dad is questioning it. When he isn't talking about football, he's talking about how he can't understand why his only daughter isn't married already."

I don't answer as I pull into the drive-through of the BBQ restaurant. I collect my thoughts and tell myself to calm down while we wait in line. I'm livid that my father thinks I have to be married at the age of twenty-five. Why can't he just be content that I'm happy with myself and am figuring out what I want to do with my life?

"Any guy who has shown interest in me has done so because of who Dad is. For once, it would be nice for someone to want me for me. Until that happens, I'll stay single. Do you have a problem with that?" I narrow my eyes at him, challenging him to say that he does. My fist will have no problems connecting with his nose if he does.

"Don't you think Colt and I wonder if people are interested in us for our talent and not because we're his sons? Of course I understand what you're going through and I have no problems with you staying single. Hell, you could become a nun for all I care." I smile at his nun comment, despite being taken aback by his admission. I didn't think my brothers were bothered by being in our daddy's limelight. I thought they loved it, so I'm surprised to hear that they too question people's motives and interests when it comes to them.

"You know, you would probably be the hottest nun alive. You in a nun's garb would spark a whole new wave of men's fantasies in Bear Creek. Maybe you should seriously consider that as your next Halloween costume." I playfully punch him in his rock-hard abs, shaking my head at where his mind goes. His eyes are gleaming with mischief, making me see how truly handsome he is. I feel bad for all the ladies that are already falling for him.

"I'm sorry I embarrassed you tonight, Carson. I just wanted him to get the hint that he'll never have a chance with me. I probably delivered it a little too harshly," I confess before driving us up to the intercom. I place our order and continue to drive forward to wait our turn.

"That's an understatement! You were brutal." He rakes his hands through his hair and sighs. "It's okay, I still love you. In all seriousness, I do want you to be happy, Adeline. Promise me you'll never settle for anyone who doesn't make you happy? Especially if Mom and Dad pressure you into it?"

"Wait, is there something I should know about? They aren't trying to do an arranged marriage with another former football player's son are they?" I wouldn't put it past my father to do something like that so I'm dead serious when I ask Carson this question.

"No, he isn't planning an arranged marriage, although now that you mention it, Dad would do something crazy like that if you aren't married by thirty." I groan at his words because he's probably right and I better get the heck out of dodge soon.

"Please don't even put that idea in his head by asking if he would ever do that."

We laugh together at the mental image as I pull up to the drive thru window to collect our food. Even though I initially didn't want to pick up my brother tonight, I'm glad my dad forced me into it. It has been a while since I had one-on-one time with Carson and hearing that we have a lot of the same concerns about trusting people makes me feel better. Hopefully after tonight, Carson will talk some sense into our parents, especially our father. Maybe, just maybe, they'll leave me alone for the time being.

I'll never settle for someone just to be in a relationship. I'm learning that I don't need to have a man to take care of me. I quite like that I can take care of myself emotionally, financially, and physically. Besides, I have a feeling that the love of my life isn't from Bear Creek. Tessa and I have plans to get out of Bear

Creek and move to Austin once her books make her more money than her current job at the rodeo. When we're settled and living in Austin, I'll warm up to the idea of dating. I already have a list of pre-requisites that my future dates must check off before I even say yes to going out with them:

They better be cute … at least in my opinion.

They better not be from Bear Creek.

They better be taller than me.

They better have a job.

They better not like football.

And they especially better not know who my father is.

# Chapter 3

## Ryan

I WAS NEVER one who took naps before we came to America, but I have learned within these last seven months of being on the road, backseat naps in the car are mandatory. Our schedule on the circuit is brutal, far worse than what we experienced in Australia and Spain. We had an inkling it was going to be taxing, especially if we wanted to make it to Nationals. But until you're actually doing it, you can't even begin to imagine how draining it is, both mentally and physically.

I open my eyes and stare at the ceiling of the rental car. I wish I was on an airplane right now instead of this cramped backseat, but our next rodeo was within driving distance from our last one. Texas is a huge state and lots of these rodeos are in smaller towns. We have a slight break coming up while being here that's appearing at the perfect time. Our bodies are hanging on by a thread before being seriously injured. We need rest, relaxation, and good food.

I also need a woman.

*Fat chance that is going to happen!*

My mood immediately blackens at the thought. I have done the unthinkable—I haven't touched a woman since we landed. With the way Rhett set our schedule, I've even been too tired for my own hand to relieve me. All we do is compete, travel, eat and sleep. And with Rhett watching my every move, I don't see any beautiful American women in my future.

My stomach rumbles, bringing my thoughts back to my current situation of hunger. I look out the window to see that dusk is settling in, making me wonder how long we've been on the road for and if we're ever going to stop driving.

"Can we please stop for dinner soon? I'm starving!" I whine when a hunger pain ricochets through my stomach. I don't care where we are at this point—I need food. Hangry Ryan is starting to rear his ugly head.

"We only have thirty minutes left until we reach the hotel. Can you wait or are you going to pass out on me like a pansy?" Rhett responds, a smirk playing on his lips when he looks at me in the rearview mirror.

Thirty minutes sounds suspiciously like one more hour to me. I have no choice but to wait since he won't pull off the road for food if we are that close.

"Fine," I groan, not liking that I have to wait. "We need to strategize this better for next year. I'm fucking tired." There's no way we can sustain this type of schedule and dominate the pro rodeo circuit.

"I was just thinking the same thing," Rhett flashes a smile while glancing back at me. "Let's talk more at dinner about how we're going to maximize our winnings by which rodeos we choose and how to minimize our traveling expenses for next year." I nod at him, my eyes gazing back out the window.

Once we started to compete and people saw how talented we really were, sponsors started to pay attention and offered us their sponsorship to help pay for our travel and registration fees. We still have a long way to go with gaining more sponsorship support. Our desire to make as much money as we can is part of our driving force. Fortunately, we both saved while we took that year and a half off helping out on the farm. Any money we've made so far has gone right back into funding this tour.

My thoughts are interrupted when I feel the vibration of my phone in my pocket. I pull it out to see I have a text message from Cody Burr, one of the cowboys we've been competing with. Cody is a great guy and has taken it upon himself to try to help us anytime we're at the same rodeo together, which has been wonderful since we don't know who to trust. We've heard plenty of stories of who the assholes of the circuit are and because of that, we've kept to ourselves. There are cliques in the pro rodeo just like anywhere else and with us being fresh competition, some of the other cowboys haven't been so welcoming. It would be nice to hang out with someone who seems trustworthy.

"Hey, are we near Austin?" I ask, praying that we aren't too far away. "Cody just sent me a text saying they're eating dinner downtown and that if we're close, we should join them. Can we? We've been snotty pricks by not socializing with anyone so far." I reason, hoping that Rhett sees the importance of us socializing with some of the guys.

"You're right, we should stop and take him up on his offer. Find out where he is so we can put it into the navigation."

I text Cody back and within seconds, he sends me the address of the restaurant. I put it into the navigation for Rhett and fortunately, it says we're only fifteen minutes away. It takes a while to find parking, but once we do, we quickly make our way into a restaurant on Austin's famed 6th Street. The restaurant is packed, but Cody and his friends stick out with their cowboy hats on. I laugh and shake my head at how goofy they look amongst the crowd. This is not a country bar. This is a trendy restaurant that features anyone but cowboys. I'm happy that Rhett and I don't wear our hats outside of work. Sure, I love the attention from the ladies, but I can get that without wearing a hat.

We make our way through the crowd to the bar where Cody and his crew are sitting. Cody is with three other cowboys from the circuit — Tate Reynolds, Luke Reno, and Casey Jennings. All three men are extremely talented and have been respectful to Rhett and me since the day we arrived. We greet everyone with handshakes and settle in, placing our drink orders with the bartender and taking a seat. While we wait, I decide to look around and check out the view.

And when I mean look around, I don't mean at the restaurant decor.

This place is crawling with gorgeous women, so much so that I decide to double up on my drink order because a plan is starting to form in this brilliant brain of mine. If I can get Rhett drunk and have some pretty little thing distract him, I can finally get some female attention that I so desperately deserve. The bartender serves us our drinks and I place a glass of Guinness against Rhett's chest, drawing his attention away from whatever he was looking at. With his back facing me while he people watches, I decide this is the perfect opportunity to involve Cody in my plan.

"Hey Cody, I need to talk to you." I make sure my voice is firm, but not loud enough for Rhett to hear what I'm about to say. "I need your help with distracting Rhett's attention away from me tonight."

"How do you mean?" he asks, his eyes squinting in confusion.

"Rhett has this horrible idea that we need to be celibate during competition. Some bullshit that it will help us focus better and that girls are just distraction, blah, blah, blah. This is the longest I've gone without having me a lady and it's really messing with me. So I was thinking, since this is our first night out and all, that maybe you and the boys can play wing men and help show Rhett a good ol' Texas time?" I wiggle my eyebrows at him, hoping he gets the hint at what I need him to do for me.

"So you want me to babysit your older brother while you go out and try to get laid tonight?" He gives me a skeptical look, as if he doubts my ability in charming a woman that quickly. I have a huge advantage over every other good-looking bloke in this bar—my Irish accent.

"That's exactly what I need you to do," I confirm, causing him to laugh at my serious tone. "This is no laughing matter, Cody. This is a cruel and unusual punishment my brother is putting me through."

"Actually, I think your brother has a point. Not that I'm saying not to have sex while you're on tour, especially if you already have a significant other, but you definitely don't want to be messing around with some of these ladies." My mouth falls open in shock, not believing what I'm hearing from him. He chuckles at my expression and shakes his head at me.

"Gentlemen, back me up here. This young stud is complaining about no sex during competition. Tate, you're the single one of out of all of us, what's your take?" Tate Reynolds is the poster child of your stereotypical good-looking, all-American guy and is a fan favorite with the ladies. Yet, I never see him with anyone. I need to find out what his deal is when I'm not knee deep in Operation: Getting Laid.

"If I'm not dating someone, then yeah, no sex with randoms during circuit season, especially girls from the rodeo." All three of them nod their heads in agreement and I feel my chances of any help with Rhett slipping away from me.

"You know, we all heard that you were a bit of a man whore before you got here and since we haven't seen that type of behavior from you, we chalked it up to just being malicious gossip. Now I know your handler over here has a muzzle on your balls." Cody slaps me on the back while the other guys laugh. "Ain't that right, Rhett?" Cody yells over to Rhett, who doesn't acknowledge him.

"Rhett! Are you listening to us?" I yell, surprised that he didn't chime in with Cody's joking. He glances back at me, but not before his eyes venture back to a table close by him.

"Clearly someone else has his attention. Who are you looking at?" All four of us follow his line of vision to see two beautiful women talking adamantly to each other. My eyes are immediately drawn to the blonde, whose gorgeous smile temporarily renders me speechless. She's speaking rapidly to her friend in excitement, her eyes wide and shining with happiness. No wonder my brother was staring at them.

*Oh shit, is he interested in the blonde?*

I've never competed with my brother for a woman's attention and I pray that tonight won't be the first because this woman is exactly what I'm looking for. Rhett and I have only been out together in a socialized setting maybe a handful of times and of those times, I was already zeroed in on my next guaranteed good time. With him and I having different tastes in lifestyles, this was never a conflict before.

"Tate, doesn't the brunette look familiar?" Cody mentions out loud and I see my brother's demeanor immediately change. His body tenses and he now gives our conversation his undivided attention. *Thank goodness, he likes the brunette!* His sudden change of behavior is probably because he has a non-negotiable rule of not dating anyone who has been with someone he knows. If he finds out she has dated one of the cowboys on the circuit, he will immediately lose interest.

"She does look familiar. I bet she's a buckle bunny." Buckle bunny is code for groupie. Disappointment is written all over Rhett's face and I actually start to feel bad for him. It's his stupid rule, but I get why he has it. I look back over at the girls, who haven't even looked our way once yet. If they were rodeo groupies, I would think by now they would've noticed us, especially Cody and the boys with their cowboy hats.

"Ah, I remember now! She works at Bear Creek Rodeo. Her name is … Tessa! Tessa Mandel! She's Caldwell George's assistant," Tate confirms and my brother's face lights up like a Christmas tree. I stare at him, not seeing this reaction from my brother in a very long time.

"I wouldn't get your sights set on her, Kearney. She makes it crystal clear to any man who even comes near her that she isn't interested." Rhett smiles at Cody, the look in his eyes telling me he's intrigued by the challenge.

"Ryan, is Bear Creek Rodeo on our schedule?" Rhett asks while his eyes are trained on the brunette.

"Yes, it's on our schedule," I confirm, amused at seeing my brother this way. It makes him look like old Rhett—happy with a touch of softness to his handsome face.

"I think it might be best if I go introduce myself to Miss Mandel ahead of time." He looks over at us and actually winks, causing the boys to slap his back with encouragement.

*My brother just winked at us!*

*Who is this man?*

"Want my hat?" Casey offers up his hat, which Rhett politely declines while putting his beer down on the bar.

"I don't need a cowboy hat to get a woman," he declares and turns his back on the hooting and hollering that is coming from the boys. I stare at my big brother in awe and realize I don't need these guys to distract my brother in order for me to meet the ladies.

Rhett is leading me to the exact one I have my eyes set on. With him being interested in her friend, this should be an easy win.

*Game. Set. Match!*

# Chapter 4

## Adeline

I HAD A feeling tonight was going to be special. That we were genuinely going to have a reason to celebrate something besides being badass babes.

Tessa's new book is a best seller.

With these sales, she will now exceed her monthly salary that she brings in from the rodeo. Meaning, our dream of moving to Austin will soon become reality.

I want to scream with excitement for her and for us!

"How much money do you think you're making right now?" I wonder, not being able to contain my curiosity on the actual figure. Millions of books are sold on that website and her book is in the top 100.

Mind blown.

"I don't know. Just because I'm #1 in a category doesn't mean it's bringing me sales."

"You're ranked in the top 100 in the whole entire store. Do you understand that? Top 100 out of millions of books!" I scream with excitement, not caring about the looks we're getting from people around us. She continues to stare at me as if I'm the crazy one, making me want to shake her until she realizes what a major accomplishment this is. I knew it was only a matter of time before this would happen. She's been hustling hard, writing when she gets home from work at night, sometimes staying up until three in the morning to finish a story, and then gets up to go to her full-time job. This is her dream career and she deserves for it to finally happen.

"That's it, Tessa, we're celebrating. We're getting rip roaring drunk and eating whatever the hell we want. We deserve to celebrate!" I exclaim, waving at our waiter to get his attention. She laughs at me while I order us a bottle of champagne.

"Did you take a screenshot of your rank yet?" When she shakes her head no, I stare at her in disbelief. "Tessa, get your phone out now and take a screenshot! You want to document this moment!" I'm always telling her to take a photo of the lowest rank she reaches since it changes hourly, but she usually waves me off as if it's no big deal.

It *is* a big, freaking deal!

This might mean our dreams of getting out of Bear Creek will happen sooner rather than later. If my calculations are correct, we might be able to start looking for an apartment in Austin as soon as the rodeo is done. Which also means I will have to tell my parents. The realization sends a wave a nausea through me. My father has a car dealership in Austin that I'm praying he will let me work out of. He isn't going to be happy and I'm dreading the conversation we need to have. Unfortunately, my graphic design services aren't supplementing my income from work yet.

But one day, they will.

Until then, I need my job with my dad, but tonight, I don't need to be worrying about my upcoming conversation with him. Tonight is all about Tessa. My thoughts become distracted when the waiter comes around with our champagne. He pours it into two flutes and leaves the rest of the bottle in a bucket of ice on our table. I raise my glass to for a toast.

"To Tessa, my best friend, my inspiration, my sister from another mister! Congratulations to you on this huge accomplishment! You're going to be an international best-selling badass author babe and I'm honored to be your forever assistant." She laughs at me, because she knows it's the truth. "Thank you for having me on this journey with you and never doubt your self-worth. You deserve all of this and more!"

"I love you, Adeline Murphy," she says, tears threatening to leak down her cheeks. "Thank you for always believing in me and we deserve this!"

I salute her with my glass and take a long pull of champagne, enjoying the smoothness of the liquid as it cools down my throat. I put my glass down and watch Tessa, who looks like she's about to lose it in the middle of the restaurant. I'm about to make fun of her for being a cry baby when her eyes go wide and her mouth opens slightly, her expression turning to a look of awe as she's captivated by something over my shoulder. I turn around to see a gorgeous man walking in our direction, his eyes locked with Tessa's. He's tall, with dark blond hair buzzed on the sides and spiked on the top, wearing a form-fitting black t-shirt that accentuates his muscular body. His dark denim jeans fit snugly and he's wearing stylish black ankle boots. I look back at Tessa, who seems to have stopped breathing as her eyes drink him in.

"Breathe, Tessa. I promise you he isn't a figment of your imagination." She doesn't even look my way when I talk to her. I chuckle and sit back, thoroughly enjoying watching her reaction to him. The man oozes sex appeal and as I look around, I notice other women's heads are turning to stare at him as well.

I grab my phone, hoping I have time to take a photo of her face, but a text message from my brother distracts me from my purpose. Before I know it, the Adonis is at our table, standing right next to Tessa. He smiles politely at both of us, but his attention is drawn right back to her.

"Excuse me ladies for interrupting your dinner, but I had to meet the woman who has the most beautiful smile I've ever seen and a laugh that is music to my soul."

I slap my hand over my mouth to stifle my outburst of laughter. That has got to be one of the cheesiest pick-up lines I have ever heard. It doesn't even make the top five worst list, but it's pretty bad. The only thing saving him right now are his good looks and yummy foreign accent. Tessa doesn't even seem to have noticed as she continues to stare at him with a deer in headlights expression. I can't tell if she's scared or in awe of him. Her eyes travel down to his lips and suddenly, her cheeks become very red. She gulps and brings her now dilated eyes back up to his.

I can't help the mischievous smile that spreads across my face as I look at her. Tessa is attracted to this guy — so much so that she seems visibly uncomfortable. I wish I can rub my hands together in glee as my plan to play matchmaker starts to form. I just hope this guy is worth it, because if he isn't, she'll chew him up and spit him out real quick.

Regardless, I'll be entertained either way.

"Tessa, aren't you going to say thank you to this kind gentleman?" I chide, pretending to look at her as if she's a crazy lunatic when on the inside, I'm dying of laughter.

"Right." She clears her throat and gives her head a quick little shake to get control over herself. "I'm sorry … and um, thanks."

*Um, thanks? Oh, she's got it bad!* I bite down on the inside of my cheek to contain my laughter. *This is going to be so much fun!*

"No, I'm sorry, I sounded like a total creeper just now. What I meant to say is that your beauty and laughter caught my attention and I just had to come over to say hello. Also, I heard your friend say in excitement something about an orange flag and your reaction to it was priceless. So, what does an orange flag mean?" He cocks his head to the side, causing Tessa to bite her lip. I really wish I had a play-by-play of what's going on inside that beautiful head of hers.

She finally looks over at me and I raise my eyebrows at her, daring her to tell him the truth about what she does and what that orange flag means. Tessa keeps her author life very private and no one in Bear Creek even knows she writes as T.M. Rose except for me. My parents know she's an author, but they have no clue what her pen name is. She prefers to keep it that way and I would never betray her trust by telling anyone. She shifts uncomfortably in her seat and I can see the wheels turning behind those aquamarine eyes, grasping for an answer.

"An orange flag is what the referees throw out at football games," she responds, making me snort out loud from her pathetic response. Mr. Sexy Foreigner smiles at her, amusement lighting up his eyes while he gives her a wicked smirk. He starts to laugh and Tessa once again freezes up and stares at him, but this time her stare has a hint of lust to it.

"If I'm not mistaken, it's a yellow flag that they throw in American football games." Clearly this guy has a sense of humor, but I wonder where he's from if he's calling it "American" football. His accent is deceiving. I can't tell if he's from Britain or Australia. Both don't seem quite right and I'm intrigued to find out more on this mystery man who has rendered my best friend speechless.

"Oh for crying out loud, Tessa! He's harmless!" I say, clucking my tongue at her for being rude and not answering his question truthfully. I give him my undivided attention, ignoring her when I feel her foot tapping my shin in warning to keep my mouth shut. "This amazing woman right here is an author and an orange flag means she's a best-selling one to boot!"

I gasp out loud at the sudden pain that explodes in my shin from her hard kick underneath the table. *I can't believe she just did that!* I narrow my eyes at her, mentally sending her a warning that she will most certainly pay for that later. I'm not certain quite yet what payback will be, but I know for sure it will be good.

"Wow, you're an author? That's remarkable. Congratulations!" He looks at her with even more interest. "What type of author are you?" He continues his line of questioning, not hiding the fact that he's impressed by her.

Hot damn, this guy wants Tessa and seems to have no problems dropping subtle hints about it.

I'm now on Team Sexy Foreigner.

"What's your name, Miss Best-Selling Author?" he asks in such an adorable way that even Tessa can't stop herself from giggling like a giddy teenager meeting her celebrity crush. She places her hand in his and just seems to stare it. I roll my eyes and decide to answer for her, not giving her a chance to lie about her name either. Lots of times we'll give out fake names to guys we aren't interested in, but there's no way in hell I'm letting her ruin it with this guy. Knowing her the way I do, bitter, angry-at-men Tessa will show up and she'll completely shut this guy down and kick him to the curb. Tessa's ex did a complete number on her, making her a bit of a man-hater these past couple of years, especially against cowboys since that's what he was. Just another reason why she wants to leave Bear Creek Rodeo

"Her name is Tessa. What's your name, Mr. Sexy Foreigner?" I give him a wink to know that I'm on his side.

"So wait, you are Tessa Mandel?"

She immediately freezes and frowns at him. She looks at me and I'm just as shocked as she is that he knows her name.

"How do you know my last name?" she questions, looking back and forth between him and I.

"My buddies over there know you. Said you work for Bear Creek Rodeo. You are an author and work at the rodeo?" We look to see who he's referring to and my stomach drops at seeing some guys from the rodeo. All of them wave at us and give Tessa a thumbs up.

I have a sinking suspicion that the night just took an unfavorable turn for Mr. International Hottie.

"Yes, I work at the rodeo," she says hesitantly, looking at me with fear in her wide eyes. I know exactly what she's thinking— this stranger now knows she's an author *and* he's friends with people associated with the rodeo. Her eyes turn a little desperate as she covers both of their hands with her free one. "Please, they don't know I'm a writer. Please don't say anything," she pleads with him, her eyes begging for him to keep silent. I lean in closer to try to hear his response, but the scraping of a chair against the floor grabs my attention and before I know it, some strange guy is sitting right next to me.

Some strange *hot* guy!

"Hello gorgeous," he purrs, giving me a smile that would rival the Cheshire cat because he looks like he's ready to devour me. Normally I would be creeped out by such a smile, but on him, he can smile that way at me anytime he wants. I look around real quick to make sure I'm not mistaken that he's talking to me and no one else. This man has got be one of the most magnificent looking men I've ever laid eyes upon. He's super model worthy and from the way he's ravishing me with his eyes and that smile on his face, he knows how good-looking he is.

*Ugh, why do I attract the cocky assholes?*

"My name's Ryan, what's your name?" He's looking me straight in the eye with bright emerald green eyes and a sense of déjà vu flashes before me. I've seen these eyes before, but I can't recall where. His eyes are so unusually bright that you can't help but stare and get sucked into their abyss.

*Snap out of it, Adeline! Don't fall into his trap!*

"I didn't ask what your name is, nor did I give you permission to sit next to me." I smile sweetly at him and silently count down the seconds to see how long it takes for him to scram. To my surprise, his smile only widens and I swear I can see the devil dancing in those eyes.

"I don't recall needing your permission, seeing as we're in the land of the free and all." My mouth drops open as he dishes it right back to me exactly the kind of sass I just gave him. I can't even think of a quick comeback before I hear additional voices at our table.

"Fancy seeing you here, ladies. Tessa, I see you've met our new friend," Tate Reynolds says, throwing his arm around Mr.

Sexy Foreigner's shoulders. Casey Jennings and Cody Burr flank each side of him and tip their hats at me in greeting. "You boys sure do move quickly," Tate laughs, looking between us and the two new guys. *How does Tate know them?*

"Where did you two meet?" Tessa asks and as I glance at her man for his answer, I quickly do a double take when I take note of his clothing and see that it's very similar to the clothing on the nice, hard, muscular body of the handsome stranger sitting next to me.

*What in the hell is going on here?*

"Tessa, do you not realize who you're talking to?" Tate asks her, but Mr. Sexy Foreigner answers for her by shaking his head.

"Well, let's not waste another minute longer. Tessa, this is Gerard Butler. Gerard, Tessa Mandel." Everyone but Tessa and I laugh at his joke because Mr. Sexy Foreigner looks nothing like Gerard Butler. I don't understand why they think it's so funny.

*Why do guys think they're funnier than they really are?*

"Personally, I think I should be the one called Gerard Butler since I have his coloring more than my brother does. I'm referring to the younger, buff Gerard Butler in the movie *300*," my hot stranger responds with a wink and it dawns on me that his accent is just like Mr. Sexy Foreigner's. When Tessa's man glances my way, I gasp when I notice the same emerald, green eyes I just encountered with the fine specimen next to me.

Brothers.

"In all seriousness, Tessa, you've been talking to the Irish Cowboy this whole time! I know you know who I'm talking about now, right?" Tate asks her, but instead of responding to him, she looks over at me, disappointment blazing out of her eyes at the realization of who he is.

Cowboys … from Ireland.

These guys are the famed Kearney brothers who came all the way here to compete in the Pro Rodeo. Tessa told me that they're all anyone can talk about right now, taking the tour by storm and selling out rodeos like hot cakes. They're also a huge hit with the ladies, which just seems to make my blood boil.

No wonder these guys ooze arrogance! People are kissing their asses left and right, catering to their every need. Women are probably throwing themselves at the feet. Well, they're in for a rude awakening if they think Tessa and I will be so welcoming. These boys need to be put in their place and realize that they can't just get anyone they want. Usually Tessa is right there with me when doling out the sass, but she's having a hard time hiding her crestfallen face. She was really taken with this guy and the knowledge of who he is just annoys me even more.

It's time to show these boys from Ireland what a true Southern woman is made of and it's not just of sweet tea and apple pie.

They think they can come into this country and sweep us off our feet with their good looks and sexy accents?

They have a rude awakening coming and it's in the form of Adeline Murphy.

# Chapter 5

## Ryan

IT SEEMS TO me that I might be witnessing my first human tornado with the storm of emotions that are playing on this blonde spitfire's face. Our reputations must have proceeded us because these two lasses seem to know exactly who we are.

And by the look of them, they don't like it.

Tessa especially looks like she's about to cry. My brother notices her change in demeanor and leans down to whisper something in her ear. Her eyes grow to big, round saucers, her lips part and she just stares at her friend in disbelief.

"What's your brother saying to her?" her friend asks in concern.

"How the hell am I supposed to know? I'm sitting here trying to get to know you," I tell her sincerely, because it's the truth. This girl is feisty, exactly how I like them. If this is her personality normally, then her bedroom manner will be like fireworks.

"Gerard Butler? Really? You *really* think you look like Gerard Butler?" She gives me an irritated look, her voice laced with sarcasm.

"Of course I don't look like him. I'm way better looking." She rolls her eyes in disgust, the gesture so adorable that I throw my head back and laugh.

"Excuse me, gentlemen," she yells at Tate and the other guys. "Just because Gerard Butler played an Irish man in *P.S. I Love You* doesn't make him Irish. He's Scottish, you jackasses." She gives her cute little sarcastic smile at them and I can tell she's relishing in the silence that follows as they ponder whether or not she's right.

My firecracker is a smart one because she's absolutely right. Most people assume he's Irish from that movie and don't even bother looking up his nationality. Being from Ireland, we know he's not from there, but I never correct anyone when they ask if I see him around town or am related to him because I'm Irish. Especially if I'm vying for the attention of a beautiful lady.

"Seriously, Adeline? How do you even know that? Do you stalk him? Are you obsessed with him?" Tate teases her like she's his little sister.

*That better be all she is to him.*

"It seems to me that we're stuck with at least two of you boys this evening." She gives me an evil side eye and I smile, proud of myself for being the smart one of the crew and not waiting on an invite to sit down. "Why don't the rest of you pull up some chairs and join us already?" Cody and Casey find more chairs and everyone crams around the table. A waiter comes by and we order a bunch of appetizers to share.

"Hey, Ryan, did you know Gerard Butler wasn't Irish?" Tate asks me a few minutes later, clearly not being able to let go of the fact that he was wrong.

"Of course I knew that, his accent is atrocious." I smile as he laughs at my joke and I look over to see my firecracker staring at me with narrowed eyes before turning her attention back to Tessa.

"Are you finally going to tell me your name or do I have to ask one of your friends?" It's time to switch gears with this one because if I want her attention, I need to be less arrogant and more engaging. She has no problems calling me out on my bullshit, which is quite refreshing for once.

"You don't need to know my name because we'll never see each other again after tonight."

"Of course I need to know your name. What kind of gentleman would I be if I didn't know the name of the girl I plan on making sweet, passionate love to?" I bite the inside of my cheek to contain my laughter at her horrified expression.

"Wow, you're really full of yourself, aren't you?" she asks incredulously, a slow smile starting to appear on her face as she sees that I'm losing the battle of containing my smile.

"I rather be fully inside of *you.*" I try to give her my best panty melting smile, but her gagging noises ruin the moment and I burst out laughing.

"Eeeww!" she whines while laughing as well. "Do these lines really work for you back in Ireland?" We're at the point that we're laughing so hard at how ridiculous I sounded that our eyes are watering and tears threaten to spill out. I've never laughed like this with someone other than my family before and as I take a couple of deep breaths to calm down, I realize it came naturally with her.

"Pretty bad, eh? And no, these lines don't work for me back home. I was just hoping to get a glimpse of that beautiful smile of yours and hear you laugh."

She wipes the tears from her eyes, her giggles calming down to the point where she's just beaming at me. We stare at each other, my eyes drawn to her lips like magnets. Her smile is genuine, making her face look angelic. She's glowing right now and I suddenly realize that I want to make her laugh like that again.

Because that smile of hers is a ray of sunshine … a ray that I want to steal for myself and keep forever.

"Thanks for that. I haven't laughed that hard in a long time," she says with a chuckle and shakes her head to regain her thoughts. "Just for that, I'll tell you my name. It's Adeline." She holds out her hand for me to shake and I take it, engulfing it into mine. Her skin feels soft and delicate, prompting me to gently squeeze. Her hand is tiny, yet feels perfect and I don't want to let it go. She slowly removes her hand from mine and I gulp down this foreign lump of emotions that just formed in my throat.

"Adeline," I repeat, loving how easily it rolls right off my tongue. "That's a beautiful name. Where did your parents get that name from?"

"A deceased grandmother," she responds with a shrug of her shoulders, the movement causing my eyes to gaze at her clavicle and then travel down the valley between her breasts. She's wearing a V-neck, loose fitting hot pink dress that barely gives me a peek of what's underneath her bra, leaving my imagination running rampant.

*Focus on her face, Ryan, not on that goddess body of hers.*

Laughter from Casey draws our attention and we listen to a story that he's telling. Food arrives a short time later, but that doesn't stop the laughter and storytelling from all the guys about rodeo life. I sit back in my chair with a full belly, contentment washing over me. Rhett and I needed a night like tonight. We needed to socialize and surround ourselves with good people in this country we barely know. I look across at him to see he's watching Tessa like a hawk while he brings a glass of water to his lips. *Shit, he's stopped drinking alcohol.* I didn't even realize that he had. With his interest captivated on Tessa, I still might be able to get some alone time with Adeline. I glance at her to see that she's also watching Tessa. Her food is barely eaten and she has switched to water as well.

"Would you like another glass of champagne?" I ask, ready to signal the waiter to bring us another bottle. She shakes her head, a sad smile forming on her face.

"No, thanks. I have a feeling Tessa is going to need me tonight and I want to make sure I'm fully alert." I follow her line of vision to see Tessa barely able to keep her eyes open, swaying in her seat, inebriated.

"Rhett can take her home. Let's be young, wild, and carefree tonight. You and me." She doesn't look at me as if I'm crazy. Instead, I see yearning in her eyes, making me wonder if she lives some sort of sheltered lifestyle.

"I'm not going to leave my best friend with a stranger. Besides, being left alone with you would be reckless in itself." Her gaze flickers to my lips, her eyes becoming a warmer shade of brown as I see a flash of desire spark in them.

"Adeline," Rhett's deep voice shatters our moment and I can't help the groan of annoyance that escapes me. "How far away is Tessa's house? She needs to go to sleep." Tessa is beyond the point of no return. Rhett's right, it's time to leave.

"We have a hotel room for tonight and it's only a block away. Do you mind helping me get her there?" Adeline asks while standing up. I move her chair back out of her way and get up to help her.

"It was always my plan to make sure you two got home safely," Rhett responds while helping Tessa out of her seat. She gets to her feet fine, but as soon as Rhett lets go of her arm, she starts to wobble. Adeline moves to Tessa's other side to help balance her upright. With Rhett and Adeline on either side of Tessa, the only help I can offer is carrying the girls' purses and opening doors for them. I pay our tab and we bid farewell to the other guys. We walk that one block to the hotel and as soon as we stand still in the elevator, Tessa wraps her arms around Rhett and lays her head against his chest. His arms instinctively wrap around her and he rests his chin on top of her head, looking as if they're a couple in love. I give my brother a questioning look, not understanding how weird he's being. He just met this girl and already he's acting as if she's his long-lost love. The doors to the elevator open and he scoops Tessa up into his arms, carrying her as if they are newlyweds about to walk over the threshold.

"Does your brother always come to the rescue of drunk damsels in distress?" Adeline asks playfully, thoroughly enjoying the show my brother is putting on.

"Honestly, no. My brother hasn't even looked at a girl in the last two years," I tell her, hoping she will see that Tessa is in good hands when it comes to my brother since I'm the scoundrel out of the two of us. He probably doesn't even think of half the dirty thoughts that run through my mind on a daily basis.

"Wait, I've got to get a picture of this for blackmail purposes," Adeline laughs as she grabs her purse to retrieve her phone. She tells Rhett to smile and snaps a couple of photos of him holding Tessa, who remains passed out the whole entire time. Adeline leads us to their room and I can't help but watch how her delectable ass sashays down the hallway.

*So much for my plans to have alone time with her.*

Adeline stops in front of their room and opens the door for Rhett. He lays Tessa down on the bed closest to the bathroom and starts caressing her forehead while Adeline takes off Tessa's shoes. There must be a body snatcher running around because I have zero clue who this person that's in my brother's body. He stares at Tessa like a love sick puppy dog. His face looks like he's in physical pain at the thought of leaving her.

"Adeline, can you please give me her phone number?" he pleads with her, almost teetering on the edge of begging. Adeline stares so intensely at him that I'm just waiting for that gorgeous, sassy mouth of hers to tell him to bugger off. She sighs heavily and retrieves the pen and paper out of the nightstand drawer.

"Hurt my friend and I'll personally poison the next beer you drink," she threatens, looking him dead in the eyes. There's my firecracker that I've thoroughly enjoyed talking to tonight.

And I'm going to thoroughly enjoy her in the bedroom as well.

"Rest assured, I'll never intentionally hurt her," he states, taking the piece of paper that contains Tessa's cell phone number from Adeline. "Thank you for this. I'll call her in the morning."

"Fair warning, she might not pick up. Tessa is pretty adamant about not getting involved with cowboys," she sighs and moves toward the door, indicating she's ready for us to leave.

"Hey, where's my digits?" I whine as we follow her. I try to think of a way to stall us from leaving, but no good excuse is coming to me. I need to stop acting so selfish and think of Adeline. She's probably worried about her friend and won't sleep very well tonight. I should just let her go to bed, but not before I get her number. An overwhelming feeling of needing to see her again consumes me.

"You didn't properly ask for it, so therefore, you don't get it." She smiles sweetly at me, making Rhett chuckle at her brazenness as he exits into the hallway. There goes that sass of hers again and I just want to shut it up by plunging my tongue into her mouth, tasting its delicious warmth. Imagining how good she tastes starts to make my jeans feel snug in all the right places.

"You're a sassy little minx … and I *like* it!" I let her know as my gaze roams her body in appreciation, causing her to roll her eyes. Needing to see her smile one more time, I wiggle my eyebrows up and down at her and mentally pump my fist in victory when I hear that sweet giggle. With Rhett having Tessa's number, I know I'll be seeing Adeline again.

"You better start getting used to seeing me around as well, Minx." Before she even has a chance to answer, I swoop in and kiss her on the cheek as I head out into the hallway. She narrows her eyes at me and looks between Rhett and me.

"We'll see if both of you are men enough to prove it."

And with that, she slams the door in our faces.

I stare at the door, never having a lady slam one in my face before. I blink a couple of times to regain my thoughts before looking at my brother, who has a devilish smirk on his face.

"And you say *I* need lessons on how-to pick-up women?" He shakes his head at me and starts heading toward the elevator.

This wasn't how I pictured my night ending, but that's okay. Tomorrow's a new day and with a small break before our next rodeo, I'll have plenty of time to woo the exquisite Adeline into my bed.

# Chapter 6

## Adeline

BETWEEN HELPING TESSA with her bouts of throw up and dreaming of a green-eyed Lucifer named Ryan Kearney, sleep eluded me. Thankfully I took the whole weekend off from work and can sleep and be lazy.

As soon as Tessa woke up, we packed up our belongings and stopped for breakfast before heading back to Bear Creek. She looks rough this morning, her thoughts a million miles away as she thinks about how one handsome Irish cowboy rocked her world within a matter of hours. I chew my toast and wonder if Rhett has called her yet. Rhett doesn't seem like the type of man who plays games by waiting to call a girl he's interested in.

*Don't lie to yourself, Adeline ... you not only want him to call to prove to Tessa that he's serious about her, but you also want an excuse to see Ryan again.*

"Have you checked your phone yet?" I casually ask in between bites. She looks up at me, her eyes questioning why I would even ask that. "To see if Rhett called," I tell her in my "duh" kind of voice because why else would I ask if she's checked her phone.

She shakes her head and continues concentrating on her food. "I didn't give him my phone number so how could he call?"

"I gave him your phone number!" I reveal in exasperation, needing her to check her phone because the suspense is killing me. *If he has called, I wonder if I can convince Tessa that we need to see the boys again tonight?*

"Why would you do that? You know I won't date cowboys."

There she goes again on her anti-cowboy stance. Sometimes hearing how much she hates cowboys is exhausting, especially when she knows not all cowboys are bad guys.

"I gave him your phone number because he wasn't going to leave our hotel room without it *and* I've never seen you react toward a man like the way you did to him," I emphasize, needing her to be honest with herself.

She shrugs her shoulders nonchalantly as if her reaction last night to him was no big deal.

It was a *huge* deal! Tessa Mandel never goes quiet and all googily-eyed over guys. Not since her ex-boyfriend shattered her heart into a million pieces and made her question every single guy's motive for looking her way. Now she's met a guy who is completely enamored by her and she's going to sit there and make excuses, acting as if it was nothing?

"Cut the bullcrap, Tessa. This is me you're talking to. You felt something way more than lust for him. He rattled you," I respond sternly, annoyed with her for not acknowledging her feelings.

She shakes her head at me, her lips in a tight, straight line in annoyance. "Yeah, he rattled me, okay? In the most uncomfortable, yet delicious way. How can a stranger evict such intense feelings out of me? It's got to be just from lack of attention."

I understand what she's saying because although Ryan didn't render me speechless like Rhett did to her, he still made me feel things that no one has ever made me feel. I've never felt such intense lust for someone, nor have I ever had the crazy dreams I had of him doing very dirty, naughty things to me.

"What did he whisper in your ear? Do you remember? I wish I could've taken a picture of your face. You mouth was so wide open from shock that bees were getting ready to make a new hive inside of it."

Her eyes go wide for a brief second before she tries to mask her reaction at remembering. "No, I don't remember." She has always been a horrible liar.

"Tessa, you get hit on all the time at the rodeo, so you can't say it's from lack of attention. There's a reason you reacted the way you did. Maybe he's the one?" She looks at me in disbelief and even I'm surprised that I just uttered those words, that I even dared to believe it's a possibility. But as I get older, I can't help but want to believe that it is. I've always been guarded with my heart because most guys who've shown interest in me have always had an agenda of what my family can do for them. I'm not as bitter as Tessa is about love, maybe because I've not opened up my heart to risk getting broken, but I refuse to believe that all men have an ulterior motive. Not everyone knows who my daddy is—I just need to find the ones who want me for *me*.

"I think you've read too many love stories, Adeline. Besides, he's exactly the type of person I don't want to date."

"Who cares if he's a cowboy, Tessa! Not all cowboys are the same." I continue with my reasons as to why she needs to give Rhett a chance, even telling her that it doesn't matter if he lives in Ireland. Either he can move here for her or she can move there, although that would really suck and I prefer she doesn't leave me. Besides, if he's going to continue competing in the Pro Rodeo, most of his time will be here in the States.

She stops arguing back against all of my points and I decide to let the matter go. It's her life and if she's too scared to take a chance on this guy, then that's her prerogative. I just have this feeling that Rhett would be *really* good for Tessa. He's just like the kind of guys I like in my romance novels.

Hot alpha males making it known that you're theirs.

Ryan made it very clear that all he's interested in was getting in my pants. Total opposite of how his brother reacted to Tessa. Rhett was a respectable gentleman, whereas Ryan acted more like a dog in heat.

A really cute dog in heat whose puppy dog eyes suck you into their naughtiness.

"Enough with your valid points. I'm too hungover to think right now, but I will say, I personally think you're trying to get me to give Rhett a chance just so you can see his handsome brother again." She gives me a smirk, knowing full well that's exactly what I'm trying to do. "Tell me, what was Ryan like?"

"Ridiculously hot with a very wicked mouth on him. You can tell he's smart with his quick one-liners and comebacks. He wasn't afraid of my sass and was even able to dish it right back to me. He wasn't scared of me … and I really liked that," I sigh, clips of our conversation from last night playing on repeat in my brain. Most guys run can't handle it when I dish them some spice, but Ryan seemed to thrive on it. His eyes brightened in excitement every time we verbally sparred.

"Whoa, I don't think I've ever heard you talk about a guy this way before," she exclaims with a surprised smile on her face.

"Because I've never met a guy like this before. He's beautiful, smart, talented and funny." The more I talk about Ryan, the greater my desire is to see him again.

"You just called a guy beautiful … are you feeling okay?" she jokes, placing her hand on my forehead to see if I have a fever. It might sound silly to call a guy beautiful, but I can't help it. Ryan is beautiful to me, in a manly, beautiful sort of way.

"Beautiful, gorgeous, hot … it all describes Ryan. Don't you feel that way about Rhett?" I question in concern, because if she doesn't feel that way about him then my chances of seeing Ryan are slim to none.

"He's the most breathtaking man I've ever seen," she sighs. "You keep asking if Rhett has called me, but you haven't mentioned if Ryan has called you yet."

"He hasn't because I never gave him my phone number."

"He didn't ask for your phone number? I'm surprised! From what I can remember, he seemed so into you."

"Oh, he asked for it, but I refused to give it to him." I can't help but giggle out loud at the memory of his shocked expression when I told him I wouldn't give it to him. I bet no girl has ever said that before.

"What? I'm so confused right now. If he asked for your phone number, why wouldn't you have given it to him?"

"Because he didn't properly ask for it. He whined about not getting it after I gave Rhett your phone number. That boy probably has women slipping their phone numbers into his jean pockets all the time without asking for it. I want him to *properly* ask me for mine."

"Don't you think you're being a little too harsh? You just met the guy and he's here for a limited time. If you really like him as much as you say you do, don't you want to spend time with him? Making him work hard for your attention might have him running the other way." Tessa looks at me skeptically, not agreeing with my decision of not giving him my phone number.

"Oh hey, pot calling the kettle black. Maybe you should be practicing what you preach, Miss Mandel." I raise my eyebrows at her and laugh when she groans and covers her face with her hands.

"I do want to spend time with him, but I don't think his intentions for me are what Rhett has for you." I give her a knowing smile, hoping she catches my meaning. "But I'm okay with that. I think it's time for some fun, so when Rhett calls you back, you will invite both gentlemen over to dinner at our house," I demand, giving her a smug smile.

Ryan Kearney has my interest peaked like no other man before. I want to know *everything* about him. What he likes, what he dislikes, why he got into bull riding.

What those full lips feel like against mine.

The way he was looking at me last night, I know I could've

had a taste of him. Molten lava rushed straight to my core every time he looked at me with his heated gaze. That man is not afraid to show when he wants someone and if I really wanted, all I had to do was say the word and he would've been mine for the evening. I can tell he's used to women falling over themselves to get his attention. I know I was a challenge to him, but I don't want to be just like any other woman to him.

I want him to want me so badly that he doesn't even look at any other woman that crosses his path.

Hope he's ready, because I'm about to give that sly fox a chase that he'll never forget.

Now I just need to remember to keep my heart intact and not fall for the playboy cowboy.

"I most certainly will *not* invite them over dinner. That's if he calls me," she huffs, making me want to shake some sense into her. "And would you seriously have sex with someone you just met?"

"I've already met him once, so it's not classified as a one-night stand anymore." I give her a wink so she knows I'm joking before I get a huge lecture on STDs and the danger of just sleeping with random guys. I've only been with one guy so far and the sex wasn't mind blowing, but it did leave me curious for more. Too bad I found out he was only dating me to get in with my family.

"Seriously, life's too short to never say never, but no, I'm not interested in being another notch on his belt buckle." She nods her head in agreement and we fall into compatible silence for the remainder of the drive home.

"Have you checked your phone?" I repeat when we pull into the parking lot of our apartment. She gives me an annoyed look and starts rummaging through her purse to find it. I hold my breath in anticipation, praying that there's a voice message from Rhett. She pulls it out and tries to turn it on, but nothing happens.

"It's dead. I'll charge it when we get upstairs."

I try to hide my disappointment behind a smile as we get out of the car and head to our apartment. Once inside, I watch her plug her phone into the charger in the kitchen and go into her bedroom, shutting the door behind her. I start a load of laundry and contemplate taking a nap, but my mind is in overdrive with thoughts of Ryan. I need a distraction, so I grab my laptop and start working on my new business logo. An hour into my work, a buzzing noise coming from the kitchen catches my attention. I get up to investigate and discover that Tessa has two missed voicemails and texts. All from a really long, foreign number. This has to be Rhett since Tessa doesn't know anyone else outside of the country. I softly squeal and do a little dance, excited to see that he's calling her. I take her phone to her room and am about to knock on her door when I realize she hasn't been out since we got home. I softly open her door to discover that she's sleeping. I glance at my watch to see that it's early afternoon. I'll give her a couple more hours of sleep before waking her up to call him back. I close her door and put her phone back in the kitchen.

The vibration of her phone interrupts me again … and again two hours later. He's called her a total of four times. Wow, this guy is persistent! Part of me feels bad that he's called her this much and she still hasn't returned his calls. What if he decides this is the last time he's going to call her until she calls him back? What if Tessa decides not to call him back? *What if Ryan is the one calling for me?* I throw down my laptop on the couch and run into the kitchen, answering the phone on the last ring.

It's time to take matters into my own hands.

# Chapter 7

## Ryan

"JUST WANT TO warn you, Shannon, that I've lost our brother," I tell my sister during our weekly call while waiting in the line for coffee. I order four cups of black coffee, three of them being for me and pay the cashier. American coffee is weak compared to what we drink back home and with the restless night I had, I need all the caffeine I can get. All I kept dreaming about was Adeline dressed up in different characters. First dream I remember she was Glinda the good witch from *The Wizard of Oz*, threatening to put a love spell on me. Except I told her I was ready and willing. Second dream was more of a hot for teacher kind of dream with Adeline teaching me the rules on love. Third dream was just her doing very naughty things to me, coaxing me into telling her I love her.

I woke up screaming from that dream.

Then I went and took a very cold shower and relieved myself with my hand.

Then I made the mistake of telling Rhett about my dreams, who decided to psycho-analyze them and told me that Adeline is my soul mate and my dreams were a way of my psyche trying to tell me without me freaking out.

Instead, Rhett's freaking me out.

"What do you mean, you've lost him?" Shannon asks, concern lacing her voice. "When was the last time you saw him?"

"Oh, he's physically still with me, but mentally, he's a goner. Gone is the miserable bastard we've been dealing with the past two years and in his place, is a sappy, pathetic excuse for a man who insists he's found his forever mate." The things that were coming out of his mouth this morning was mind blowing. Telling me that there's something special about Tessa and that he's determined to make her his.

"Wait, Rhett's found a girl? When did this happen? How long have they been together?" Shannon starts with her rapid fire of questions and I can't wait to hear how shocked she's going to be.

"This happened less than twenty-four hours ago. They haven't even been on one date. It was like she hypnotized him with her beauty because as soon as he laid eyes on her, he was a changed man. He was charming, engaging in conversation, and was smiling and laughing with all of us."

"They just met last night?" she questions, the tone in her voice starting to sound doubtful.

"Yes, this all happened last night at dinner and to top it all off, he has already called her two times this morning! She hasn't called him back yet, rightfully so as he's starting to look like a bit of a creeper if you ask me."

"You're talking about *our* brother Rhett?"

I chuckle at her, picturing the expression on her face. Shannon and I are only a year apart and are closer to one another than Rhett and I are. Due to our age difference, he was in a different school than us and once he started his career, was always gone. If it wasn't for the rodeo, I honestly don't know how close Rhett and I would really be with each other.

"If she doesn't call him back, I'm afraid he might go into a depression. That or I'll have to bail him out of jail for being a stalker." Depression is more of Rhett's style than jail time and I refuse to sit by and watch him make a fool over himself, especially if Tessa isn't interested.

"I can't believe Rhett has found his soulmate all the way in America."

*Wait, what?*

"Jesus, Mary and Joseph, Shannon! Don't tell me you believe this hogwash too?" I practically yell at her, not believing my ears that she drinks the Kool-Aid on love.

"Of course I believe it, Ryan. Look at our parents! They met and fell in love at first sight and look how long they've been married. Why are you so against love? Do you really want to grow old alone?"

"How can you grow old alone when this world has billions of people on it? It's called variety and adding experience to your life," I reason, believing my own bullshit that's coming out of my mouth.

"That's pathetic, Ryan. I don't wish that upon you. You deserve love and to be loved. I wish you would see that."

"But that's the thing, Shannon, millions of women *do* love me," I joke even though I have zero clue as to who any of those millions of women are.

"I have to go help Mum, but have Rhett call me later. I really want to hear more about his lady."

"He doesn't have a lady if she won't call him back. I'll be sure to tell him your message and keep you posted. Give hugs to everyone for us." I hang up with my sister, start the car, and drive back to our hotel.

I need Tessa to call Rhett back. Not only for his mental wellbeing, but because I want to see Adeline again. I kind of liked that she played hard to get last night and didn't so easily succumb to my charm. Wondering what that blonde minx tastes like has consumed my thoughts and I'm afraid it will only continue until it happens or I meet someone else to distract me.

I'm really hoping that it happens, but it won't unless Tessa calls back or picks up her phone. I worry that if Rhett continues calling her without waiting for her to return his call, he'll push her away.

As soon as I get back into the hotel room, Rhett is back on the phone, leaving another message for Tessa. I argue with him about his current disturbing tendencies and tell him to leave her alone.

"C'mon, let's go work out so we're ready for Belton this weekend," he suggests and I agree since working out will help get my mind off of Adeline for a short while. Once we are done competing in Belton, we travel to North Texas for some rodeos before coming back south to compete in Bear Creek. Just thinking about the upcoming schedule makes me groan and I'm so happy that season is almost over. We are doing very well in the standings and if season ended today, we'd qualify for Nationals. We just need to remain healthy and make the top five in our respective categories in the next rodeos to get to Las Vegas.

We workout in the hotel gym for over an hour before swimming laps in the pool. After our swim, we go back to our room to shower and get dressed. We answer some emails and Rhett finalizes more of our travel plans. By the time we're done, it's getting close to dinner and Tessa still hasn't called. My stomach won't stop growling for food and I tell Rhett that we need to grab dinner and go grocery shopping to have some food in our room since we'll be in town for the next couple of days.

"All right let me just try Tessa one more time and then we can go," he says while reaching for his phone. I grab it before he has a chance and hold it hostage.

"No! Stop the stalker madness! You are not calling her again today! What in the hell is wrong with you? You aren't even in a relationship with her. You don't even know if this girl feels the same way you do. Tessa might be a complete psychopath," I ramble on, needing to make my point so he stops making an ass of himself. I don't think I've ever called a girl four times in one day. Not even my own mother.

"Give me my phone, Ryan," he responds calmly while I shake my head at him. "You're right, I don't know who she is as a person or how she feels about me, but how else am I going to know if I don't keep trying? Besides, aren't you interested in seeing Adeline? You couldn't even charm her enough last night to get her phone number. These American girls must see through your bullshit." I hurl his phone at him, specifically aiming for his head in the hopes that it knocks some sense into him.

"Of course I want to see Adeline again, but you might be ruining our chances. It's not normal to call a woman that many times in a day, especially since she hasn't called you back yet."

"The first two times I called, it went straight to voicemail, indicating that either her phone was turned off or dead. The last two times it rang and went to voicemail. I'm sorry, but I can't help but be worried about her, especially in the condition she was in last night. I promise this will be the last call I make."

"Don't know if I believe you, so if she doesn't pick up, you agree to give me your phone to hold for the rest of the night. Deal?" I really hope she doesn't pick up this time because I want his phone so I can text her saying that I understand if she never wants to talk to my psycho brother again, but can she please give Adeline my phone number to call me?

"Deal," Rhett confirms and continues to dial her phone number. Victory is starting to taste sweet as he gets almost to the fourth ring without her picking up and then suddenly it happens.

She picks up.

But she turns out to be my little minx instead of Tessa.

"I appreciate you picking up the phone and updating me. Did she have a rough night?" Rhett asks Adeline in curiosity. I'm dying to hear what she's saying, but unfortunately, Adeline's voice is not loud enough for me to hear out of the phone. So instead I watch Rhett's facial features. His eyes go wide and he looks at me with a gleam of excitement. He thanks Adeline and tells her to text him their address.

"Adeline just invited us over for dinner. Here's your second chance to try not to be a prick for once and this time, get her phone number." I can't believe that my brother's stalker ways worked and we have a date tonight with our two beautiful Americans.

I can't wait to see what my little minx dishes out at me. Regardless of what happens, there's no way I'm leaving their place without her phone number.

And to finally taste what I've been dreaming of.

# Chapter 8

## Adeline

TWO HOURS IS all I had to get ready for the boys to come over for dinner.

As soon as I got off the phone with Rhett, I ran into my room, showered, and got myself all dolled up for this evening's company. I try to look casual with a black, off-the-shoulder form fitting top and jean shorts that show of my shapely legs, but barely cover my butt cheeks. I put heavy mascara on and keep the rest of my make-up light and neutral. I curl my hair into loose waves down my back. I scan over myself in the mirror, satisfied that Ryan should be salivating at the sight of me.

Our apartment was already clean so I just had to concentrate on getting dinner prepared. I'm a decent cook, but we had a limited amount of food in our refrigerator. I decided that fajitas would be the safest bet since I wasn't sure what these guys even liked to eat.

So engrossed was I in making sure dinner was ready for their arrival that I forgot to wake up Tessa. Fortunately, she woke up on her own, but was not very happy with me for answering her phone and especially for inviting them over without consulting her. I tuned out her arguments while I cooked because inviting them over is *exactly* what she needs.

It's exactly what *I* need.

The doorbell rings in the middle of her rant and I can't help but give her a wicked smile when she looks at me in despair and runs into her room to get ready. I count to ten, take a deep breath and walk slowly to the door. I pull it open and my breath catches at the sight of the two handsome men standing outside of it. They are both dressed casually, but their style choices accentuate their perfect rock-hard bodies. Both give me a heart stopping smile in greeting and all I can do is swallow the lump of desire that forms when I meet Ryan's eyes. Rhett comes in first, giving me a kiss on the cheek and thanking me for the invite. Ryan proceeds next, closing the door after him and stops to stand in front of me. His mouth curves into a salacious smile while his eyes rake admiringly over my body. My heart starts to hammer in my chest as he leans in slowly and grazes his lips against my cheek.

"My sexy little minx looks divine enough to be my dinner tonight," he whispers in his husky, Irish brogue, making my panties instantly wet from the visions of his mouth all over me. He pulls back and hands me a gorgeous bouquet of sunflowers. "These are for you. Their beauty and brightness reminded me of you."

I gasp and stare at him with my mouth slightly ajar, not understanding how he could have possibly known that sunflowers are my favorite kind of flower.

*Heart stop melting.*

"Thank you," I sincerely say as I grab them to put in a vase. "They're beautiful." I look over at Rhett to see that he's carrying a bouquet of Tessa's favorite flowers. *Is this some sort of sign?* I shake my head at the ridiculous thought because this just has to be a coincidence.

"Please make yourself at home. Tessa will be out shortly, she woke up late." I bring them both beers and start to set the table for dinner when Tessa finally comes out. Rhett immediately gets up to walk over to her and they're both sucked into each other's world. Ryan comes over to help me set the table, rolling his eyes at them which causes me to laugh.

Dinner starts off in awkward silence, but soon we start asking each other questions, getting to know one another better. I loved when Ryan and Rhett would talk about their childhood in Ireland, about their farm and their sister. I can almost picture how beautiful it is there from the words they used to describe it. I've always wanted to travel and I hope I can do more of it once I'm a full-time graphic designer.

Both men were impressed to hear what our goals were for ourselves and anytime the conversation veered toward the subject of my family, I tried to keep my answers as vague as possible. After dinner was completed, the men helped us clean up and Rhett announced that he was taking Tessa for a walk. This is music to my ears as I've been craving for some alone time with Ryan ever since he came through that door. Sitting across from him at dinner was almost unbearable because I couldn't stop staring at his mouth, hoping I would discover tonight what those lips feel like.

My wait is almost over.

"Have a good time, kids!" Ryan waves them off with a cocky grin before I shut the door on them, my own devious smile playing on my lips. I turn around and walk slowly over to him, the electricity in the air crackling from our sexual tension. He's sitting on my couch, one arm draped over the back of it, looking at me as if he knows what's about to come next.

I stand in front of him, staring at him with heat blazing out of my eyes. "Are you ready for dessert, Cowboy?"

His mouth slides up into a delicious, wicked smile. "Are you my dessert?" he asks as I slide onto his lap, my hands sliding up his muscled chest and setting into his hair.

"Just a taste," I whisper, my lips inching their way closer and closer to his mouth. I suddenly stop, gazing into his emerald eyes that are bright with desire. I've never been so brazen with a man before, but Ryan Kearney has set a fire inside of me that only he can extinguish. Part of me prays that his breath is going to smell, hoping all desire for him will be eliminated.

But as my lips softly start to caress his, they feel exactly as I imagined they would.

Soft, but with a silky firmness to them.

As our kiss starts to deepen and his tongue invades my mouth, his breath is as delicious as I dreamt it would be. His tongue is forceful, but in a way that ignites your senses, leaving you wanting more.

No man has kissed me the way Ryan has—his tongue commanding me with every stroke, sending sparks straight to my core. He has consumed me in a way that at some point, he maneuvered us so I'm pinned underneath him.

I didn't even notice.

I can feel his long, hard erection through his jeans and once he settles in between my legs, my body automatically starts to rub against him, the friction sending addicting waves of pleasure throughout my body, craving for more. My moans get louder, my hips moving faster, my body in a frenzy for my release. But once I feel his fingers rub against my stomach to unbutton my shorts, a cold splash of reality douses my fire. Warning bells start to go off, my brain screaming I need to slow it down or else I will just be another conquest to him.

I break free from our kiss, my hand grabbing his before he succeeds in getting my shorts off. He pulls back to look at me, our heavy breathing the only sound echoing within the apartment.

"Adi, are you okay?" he asks, calling me by my nickname. "Because you're about to make me explode in my pants with how amazing you feel underneath me." He touches his forehead to mine and kisses me softly.

"I think maybe we should slow things down," I suggest, giving him a nudge to let me up. We both sit up, his gaze hooded with want while he watches me button my shorts back up.

"Okay ... no problem." He winces as if he's in pain while he tries to adjust himself. My eyes immediately go to his erection, widening at how big it looks.

"You can't look at me that way, Minx," he laughs, raking his hands through his hair. "We'll continue where we just left off if you don't revert your eyes." He sighs and gives his head a good shake. "Talk to me. Distract me with something that's far from being sexual and no sneaky innuendos. I'm already seeing how smart that brain of yours is." He grins at me and my heart skips a beat. He looks perfect right now with his hair disheveled from my hands and his lips swollen from our kisses.

"Do you know who Clint Murphy is?" I question, my eyes turning serious as I look at him. If I'm going to continue wanting Ryan the way I want him right now, I need to find out if he knows who my family is.

*Please don't know who my father is.*

His smile slowly fades from his face and he stares at me before answering. "You're not seriously going to tell me that you have a boyfriend named Clint Murphy right now, are you?"

"God *no!*" I exclaim, the thought making me want to vomit.

"Oh, thank the lord." He breathes a sigh of relief and starts to laugh. "Wait, you don't have a boyfriend, right?"

"Do you really think I would be making out with you if I did?"

"You never know. I'm pretty irresistible." He winks and I punch him in the arm. He's right though because I'm having a hard time keeping my hands to myself right now.

"Do you like football?" I continue on, needing to get this conversation out of the way.

"Yes, I love football." His eyes light up and my heart drops.

"Who's your favorite team?" I cast my eyes downward and start to fidget with my shorts, praying that none of his favorite teams are within the state of Texas.

"The Rovers?" he says as a question, his eyes silently asking where this conversation is heading.

"The who?" I ask in surprise since I've never heard of them before.

"The Shamrock Rovers."

"Wait … are you talking about soccer?" I completely forgot that football in Europe is what we call soccer.

"Ugh, that word. I refuse to even call my beloved football that horrid name."

He looks so serious that I can't help but burst out laughing at him. I also can't help but feel relieved to know that he doesn't even watch American football.

"You're ridiculous," I tease and reach over to ruffle his hair.

He grabs my wrists, hauling me against his chest and searing me with a kiss that leaves me panting for more. "You like my ridiculousness," he counters with his signature devilish smile playing on his lips.

"Maybe I do," I whisper, realizing that if I'm not careful, Ryan could capture my heart and then shatter it when he's done with me.

*Heart, please don't fall in love with him.*

"Since Tessa doesn't seem to have a good track record with picking up the phone when Rhett calls her, can I please get your phone number?"

I giggle at him just as the door opens and Tessa and Rhett walk in. Her face is flushed, her lips red from obviously being kissed and her whole entire face is glowing. I think it's safe to say that she'll now be picking up the phone when Rhett calls her.

We stand up from the couch, our time alone together coming to an end. He programs my phone number in his phone as Adi the Minx. "Have sweet dreams of me, my little minx," he whispers in my ear when saying goodbye.

And my dreams are once again filled with a green-eyed devil doing very naughty things to me.

# Chapter 9

## Ryan

TRUE TO MY word, I call Adeline as soon as I wake up the next morning, wanting to make plans with her before the day slips away from me. She says she can only meet me for lunch because she has dinner plans with her family. She offers to come to Belton, claiming it has more restaurant options than Bear Creek does. I don't care where we go, as long as I get a chance to kiss her again.

My hope for alone time with her was quickly dashed when Rhett announced that since Tessa has to work, he's coming to lunch with us. At first, I thought he was joking, but when he said that Adeline needed someone to keep her safe from the likes of me, I knew he was serious. I was pissed at him for being a cock blocker, but as lunch progressed and I watched him make her laugh, I realized I liked the fact that they liked and respected each other.

We talked on the phone before going to bed, something that I've never done before with a woman. I asked her how her family dinner went and noticed her answers were short while not giving up much information on them. I made a mental note to ask again another time and we hung up after talking for an hour. My dreams were once again filled with her, making me wake up with an extreme hard on. I was determined that today I was going to get alone time with her. Rhett was frustrated at not seeing Tessa yesterday, so he came up with the genius idea of us surprising them at their jobs. We went to work-out, shower and then pick up more flowers for them to have in their offices. He drops me off first at Adeline's car dealership and as I watch him drive away, a part of me gets nervous and wonders what in the hell I'm doing. I've never surprised anyone at their job, let alone a girl.

My little minx is bringing out a lot of firsts for me and I don't know how I feel about it.

I shake off any doubts and stride confidently into the dealership. The receptionist tells me that Adeline is in a meeting and that I can take a seat in her office. Her office is not really private, with two glass panels walls letting everyone see inside. I sit down and look around her workspace. She has no personal belongings on her desk, only stacks of papers. Obviously, this place is just a paycheck for her and not a place she enjoys working. I can't help but smile at the mental image of how excited she's going to be when she can turn in her resignation to pursue her graphic design career.

Voices catch my attention and I turn my head to see Adeline walking out of an office, an older gentleman walking behind her. He's extremely tall and in very good shape for his age. I squint my eyes harder to see that he's also very good looking. Anger starts to bubble inside of me as I see him place his hands on her shoulders and squeeze.

*What the hell? No one should be touching her like that.*

I rise out of my seat and start to walk over, my pace quickening when I observe him engulf her in a hug, squeezing her in a way that's inappropriate at a work establishment.

"Hey!" I yell out, my voice grabbing their attention. "Get

your hands off of her!" He releases her, a shocked expression on both of their faces.

"Ryan, what are you doing here?" Adeline asks, looking nervously between myself and the older man.

"Adeline, who is this young man?" His heavy southern accent is commanding, making Adeline flinch. His powerful, well-muscled figure is encased in a three-piece suit, screaming that he's the boss of this place. His blue eyes are cold, sizing me up and down. He has a couple of inches on me in height and muscle, but I'm confident that if I need to take him down, my youth and speed will prevail.

"I saw the way you were hugging her, squeezing her so tight you can feel her breasts against your chest. That's sexual harassment." I point my finger at him, inching my way closer into his personal space.

"Ryan! That's my boss!" Adeline exclaims, trying to get in between us.

"Exactly, Adeline! He needs to be reported. No one touches you like that!" I roar, not noticing the crowd that is starting to gather around.

"He's also my dad!" Her words start to sink in and I look between the two of them, finally seeing the resemblance.

*Oh shit!*

I take a step back and swallow, my movement not going unnoticed by her father as he raises an amused eyebrow at me.

"Ryan Kearney, meet my father and boss, Clint Murphy." I look at her in shock as she reveals his name. Adeline was asking me if I knew her father, who judging by his size and build, played American football.

"It's nice to meet you, sir," I hold out my hand for him to shake. He gives me a quizzical look before deciding to take it.

"Kearney … are you one of those Celtic cowboys I keep hearing about that's coming to the rodeo?"

"Yes, sir, that would be me." I swallow down the pain I feel as he squeezes my hand as hard as can.

"How do you know my daughter?" he questions, not releasing his grip on my hand.

"Daddy, we met through mutual friends," Adeline answers for me, tapping her father's hand so he can release mine. As soon as he does, I clench and unclench my hand into a fist, trying to regain my circulation back.

"And why are you here right now? Do you need to buy a vehicle?" he asks, his question causing Adeline to roll her eyes and shake her head at him.

"No sir, I came to take Adeline to lunch."

"And are those flowers for my daughter or were you planning on hitting me over the head with them?" I look down to see a pile of the petals have fallen off the sunflowers from my rough hand gestures while I held them.

"These are for you. I'm sorry they aren't as pretty as they were when I walked in with them." I hand her the flowers and she gives me a small smile of gratitude, her cheeks flushed red with embarrassment.

"I thought cowboys were included on your list of men not to date, Adeline?" her father questions, making Adeline's cheeks turn a brighter red.

"I'm trying to change her mind on that, sir. Hoping a nice lunch might cloud her judgement and score me some points." I smile at him, the gesture not being returned back.

He looks at her, then stares at me for a couple of seconds before turning back to her. "Why don't you take an extended lunch and I'll see you back here later?"

"Thank you, sir," I quickly chime in, not wanting him to change his mind. "And I'm sorry about the earlier mishap."

"I liked that you were trying to protect my daughter, so thank you. But don't get any funny ideas when taking advantage of an extended lunch, you got that?" His voice takes on that commanding tone as he points his finger in my face. Adeline and I nod our heads and watch him walk away.

We stroll in silence to the receptionist's desk, where Adeline asks if she can put the flowers in water for her while she's gone. We head to her car and it's not until the doors are shut that I exhale the breath I was holding in.

"I'm sorry for embarrassing you, Adi, but I didn't know he was your dad and I especially didn't like how he was holding you. Why did you ask me the other night if I knew who he was? Is he famous?" I turn my body toward her, waiting for her to answer me.

She nods, but keeps her eyes straight at the windshield, refusing to look at me. "I just wanted to make sure you didn't know who he was."

"Why would it matter if I knew who he was?" I ask in confusion, not understanding if she's disappointed or not that I didn't know he played American football.

She takes a deep breath and slowly exhales it out. "I just wanted to see if you were interested in me for me and not who my dad is."

I reach over and grasp her chin, forcing her to look me in the eyes. "I didn't know who your daddy was when I met you, nor did I know who he was when I was kissing you on your couch the other night. No offense, but I couldn't give two shits about who your daddy is and what kind of career he had. If you tell me you love your daddy, then I'll be respectful to him. If you tell me you hate your daddy, then I will keep him far away from you." Tears start to well up in her eyes and I can see the pain that has come from having a famous father shine in them.

"Let me tell you what I'm interested in, Adeline. I'm interested in this." I press my index finger to her forehead, indicating that beautiful brain of hers.

"I'm interested in this." I place my finger on her lips, wanting to kiss them so badly.

"I'm interested in this." I press my finger to where her heart is, praying that I don't unintentionally hurt it.

"And I may have a slight interest in this." I tease with a sly smile, sliding my fingers down her sternum, past her stomach and stop at her entrance, praying that I get to devour that soon. She slaps my hand away with a laugh, relief washing over me seeing her beautiful smile.

"C'mon, let's go get something to eat and you can tell me all about what it's like to be Clint Murphy's daughter over lunch." I can feel that she needs to talk and quite honestly, I want her to talk to me.

I want to know everything there is about Adeline Murphy.

# *Chapter 10*

## Adeline

ONCE I LET my guard down with Ryan and told him about my feelings regarding my family, I was surprised to learn we had more in common than I thought. Ireland doesn't produce many successful professional cowboys, so Ryan and Rhett have become somewhat famous back home. Their family is also well-known for their horse farm, and while that isn't the same as being a child of a football legend, it still left them with doubt on who to trust.

"You do realize that you girls are dating guys that are kinda big deals back in Ireland, right?" I gave him a funny look, not knowing if he was being his usual arrogant self or speaking the truth.

*Wait, did he just say we're dating?*

"People just look at us and see dollar signs and the connections we have into the elite world of horse breeding, so I understand your lack of trust when meeting people. But Adi, life's too short. Not everyone is going to be after you for your family's name and money. Not everyone is going to be interested in you just because of who your dad and brothers are. You need to start letting people in. Be a little bit guarded, but give people a chance," he told me, making me wonder how he would react knowing that by me letting him in, he's starting to capture my heart.

It's not lost on me the irony that the one guy I let my guard down with is the biggest playboy of them all.

But Ryan has been acting anything but a playboy. He's made plans with me every night this week. Rhett and Tessa usually join us, which has actually been quite entertaining. We all eat dinner together, play a game that involves us getting to know one another better, and then go our separate ways to have alone time. Besides getting acquainted with each other mentally, we've been physically getting to know each other's bodies as well.

Tonight is the night before they leave for the rodeo in Belton. I'm lying back on the couch, my eyes closed and my breathing ragged as I try to come down from the most explosive orgasm I've ever had from oral sex. I knew Ryan was talented with his tongue, but he took it to a whole other level tonight. I slowly open my eyes and see him staring down at me, an expression of raw, honest hunger blazing in his eyes. I don't know how much longer I can hold off my need to feel him inside of me. Physically, that's the next step, but mentally, my head and heart are still fighting over what I should do. If this is how my heart is reacting to him without us having sex, I know he'll completely dominate me once we do.

He will own me—mind, body, and soul.

Giving that much power to a man who isn't committed to me is frightening, but what if I never feel this way again for someone? I push these thoughts aside, not wanting him to sense my inner turmoil and ask me about it.

*Not like you would tell him the truth anyway.*

"Do you have any plans this weekend?" he asks, his expression so intense that I feel like he's trying to read into my soul.

"Yes, I do," I confirm, his eyebrows shoot up in surprise at my response. "I've got a hot date with Netflix and this really comfy couch." I give him a mischievous smile while patting the cushions.

He smirks at me, grabs my hand and places it over his growing erection. "Can you feel what your sassy little mouth does to me, Minx? I want you to come with me to Belton."

My mouth drops open in surprise, not expecting an invitation from him. "Really?" He laughs at the skepticism in my voice and pulls me up into a sitting position.

"Yes, really. It'll be like a mini holiday and you can see what a stud I am on the bull." He winks before searing my lips with a hot kiss. "I haven't talked with Rhett yet, but I wouldn't be surprised if he invites Tessa."

"Tessa has to work Friday. Oh shoot," I cry out in frustration, forgetting about my family obligation. "Since I missed my brother's football game last week, I promised I would go to his game tomorrow night."

"The rodeo isn't until Saturday; we just have to attend the events the night before. What if you girls drive up Saturday afternoon? That way you can still see us ride, we can have dinner and spend the night. Not in the same room as Rhett and Tessa, of course." He smiles wickedly at me and my imagination goes wild with all the naughty things we can do in our own room.

*I'm in trouble.*

"Of course," I say in a shaky breath, gulping down my nervousness.

"So, what do you say? Will you come to Belton?" His eyes are hopeful as he waits for my response. After this, he and Rhett travel for four weeks to rodeos in Northern Texas. *What if he loses interest in me while he's away?* The thought of this being our last weekend together decides my answer for me.

"I would love to come to Belton."

I WOKE UP early on Saturday, my excitement at seeing Ryan preventing me from sleeping in. My mother was relentless with her endless questions about Ryan while we were at my brother's game last night. I thought I had pacified her with my answers long enough to leave me alone, but her questioning continued at dinner. Even though I tried to play it off as nothing serious, my mother could tell it was more than just that.

"Be careful, Adi. I don't want you getting hurt," she said.

*Too late for that!*

As soon as I got home, Ryan called and we talked about how our day went. I loved hearing how he prepares himself, both mentally and physically, for his rodeos. Even though he's been gone for only a day, hearing his voice made me realized that I missed him.

Of course, I didn't dare admit that to him!

Seeing that I have my whole day ahead of me since we don't leave until this afternoon, I get up to make coffee and start a load of laundry. I try on a couple of outfits to wear tonight, wanting to look good for him, but not too over the top. Once that's picked, it's time to decide on bedtime attire. I look through my collection of nightgowns and pull out my sexiest ones. I stare at my two options, wondering if bringing them would be insinuating that we're going to have sex. I start to get way too deep into my head about should I or shouldn't I bring them with the final decision being to bring one sexy nightgown and one set of pajama pants with a tank top.

When my overnight bag is ready, I clean the apartment, trying hard not to wake up Tessa, who didn't get home until late. I forego vacuuming and go back into my room to see it's not even lunchtime yet. With at least two more hours to kill until I need to start getting ready, I grab my laptop and research bull riding. I've only been to the Bear Creek Rodeo a handful of times and never bothered educating myself on the riders or the individual events. If I'm going to watch Ryan in action tonight, I need to at least know what all of the terminology and rules are.

Ten minutes into watching YouTube videos and my anxiety level is through the roof. How Ryan hasn't broken every single bone in his body is beyond me. Just seeing the way their bodies flap around like a fish out of water makes me dizzy. I don't know if I'll be able to handle watching him. It's one thing when you don't know the person, but when it's someone you care about, those eight-seconds of him on that bull are going to be grueling.

I click out of YouTube and go back to my main internet page. The cursor in the Google search engine box taunts me, daring me to type in Ryan's name. *Don't do it*, my mind is screaming, but my fingers seem to have made the decision for me. The first couple of articles are interviews of him and Rhett coming to America. Then there are videos of some of his rides. I continue scrolling down and click on the next page when articles from gossip columns start appearing. There are pages and pages of stories about him and all of them contain pictures of him with different women. Not wanting to be tempted to read all of them, I click on the "images" tab instead.

Big mistake.

Hundreds of photos appear of him with different women, ranging from local socialites, models, and celebrities. It's rare that I can find more than five photos of him with the same woman and the one woman who does appear in more than five turned out to be his sister, Shannon, who's gorgeous. I was relieved when I discovered it was his sister, but the more I kept digging, the more disturbed I was to see that he's never really had a serious girlfriend, that all these women were just casual flings.

And I was his next one.

I slam my laptop shut, tears threatening to spill down my cheeks. I don't know why this is so devastating to me. Tessa warned me about his reputation, even telling me that Rhett inflicted a "no-girls" rule at the beginning of their season and the only reason Ryan has stuck with it is because Rhett has been all over him about it.

I've been that one exception to the rule because of Rhett's

interest in Tessa.

I try to look at the bright side—Rhett will probably uphold this rule while the boys are away from us. But my heart wants Ryan to stay away from other women because I'm the only one he wants. Sadness invades my heart and all my excitement for tonight quickly vanishes.

I debate whether or not to feign sickness and not go, but despite my anguish, I still want to see him. I still want to gaze into those green eyes, listen to that husky Irish accent, and be tortured by the touch of his firm, warm lips.

*It's okay, Adeline, you're a strong girl. You can handle casual,* my heart sings out.

*No, you stupid twit, you cannot,* my brain yells back.

It appears that I've foolishly fallen in love with Ryan Kearney. An unrequited love that with one hundred percent certainty will devastate me.

I take a couple of deep breaths and know that deep down, I would regret not going. I start getting ready, my movements slow and hesitant, my confidence completely shattered by those images.

"You ready to go?" Tessa calls out an hour later, her face glowing with happiness at the idea of seeing Rhett again.

I plaster a smile on my face and nod with fake enthusiasm. We grab our belongings and head out to Belton.

# Chapter 11

## Ryan

I PACE BACK and forth in the holding area, waiting for my turn to compete, trying to shake off this nervous energy that is brewing within me. Rhett just finished competing and managed to nail his ride, despite being in a black mood with the discovery that Tessa's ex-boyfriend is here competing with us. I had to talk him off the ledge, which is no easy task with how hard-headed he is. I've never seen my brother so possessed with jealousy and rage before and if I hadn't held him back, he might've gotten disqualified for punching the crap out of Ty George. The wanker deserves to be punched, but we're *so close* to qualifying for Nationals that we can't let our emotions get the better of us.

Which is easier said than done at the moment.

I spend one day away from Adeline and she's all I can think about. Training for today was only a temporary distraction since she's ingrained herself into my blood, my need to have my fix of her consuming my every waking moment.

*Who the hell am I?*

No woman has ever grabbed my attention like this as she has.

Excitement and anticipation at seeing her gorgeous face got me up early and ready to start my day. As the hours started ticking by, my energy changed and I became jittery. I've never been anxious before a rodeo, but for some reason, I was antsy and moody, checking my phone for messages of her arrival, doubt starting to creep in if she was even going to show up. The feeling was so strong that relief washed over me when I did get a text saying she arrived. I've never been one to believe in intuition, but when I saw doubt and sadness reflect back at me in those chocolate brown eyes, I was hit by a massive wave of fear.

Fear that she didn't want me anymore.

This particular fear was so foreign to me, so disturbing, that it left me sick to my stomach. The only way I knew how to squash it was to kiss her. Before even speaking one word to her, I grabbed her roughly, hauled her against my chest, and crushed my mouth to hers. I didn't care that we were in public, that the other guys were making lewd comments. I needed to feel her respond to me, to feel that she still wanted me just as much as I wanted her. When I finally ended the kiss and she opened her eyes, passion and hunger were smoldering back at me. She gave me her naughty smile and I knew that I still had my little minx in my clutches.

"I missed you," I whispered to her, her eyes widening in surprise.

"I've missed you too." I didn't realize how much I needed to hear that from her until the words were out of her mouth.

I've never wanted anyone as badly as I want Adeline Murphy.

And it scared me to my core.

I'm not supposed to feel this way over someone I just met. I thrived on my reputation of being the playboy cowboy. I loved the attention, the game of seeing how many women I could get in my bed. Yet, this lass had spun my world around. All those desires of freedom to do what I want with whomever I want are gone and in their place are just desires for her.

Only her.

This obsessive need of ownership over her is a dangerous distraction, one that I must find a way to handle better. Maybe this upcoming break from seeing each other every day will do us good.

*Do me good.*

"Kearney, you're up!" My name being called breaks through my thoughts and I walk over to the chute where the bull is. I have this tradition of looking into the bull's eye and giving them a pep talk before we ride.

"Hello big fella," I say to the bull in greeting, using a soft tone of voice with him. "I've got my girl here with me, so I'd really appreciate it if you can go kindly on me." The animal blinks at me and looks away.

"Okay, well, good chatting with you. Let's go do this!" I say more to myself than to the bull while I mount it. I let my weight settle onto it's back, gain my balance and secure the rope in my grip. I take a couple of deep breaths and close my eyes, my heart hammering in my chest as I say a silent prayer for a safe and successful ride.

I imagine my victory and when I open up my eyes, focus and determination have taken over me. I nod to signal that I'm ready.

The chute doors open and the bull storms out into the arena, making me hold on for dear life for those eight-seconds.

"CHEERS TO THE Kearney brothers for dominating Belton!" Adeline cheers us in a toast at dinner. Both Rhett and I had picture perfect rides, placing first in our categories, and helping us move slightly higher in the overall money earning ranks for Nationals. The top fifteen qualify for Las Vegas and we are sitting pretty in the top ten.

Once we calmed down from the highs and lows of the rodeo, we started to relax and enjoy our celebratory dinner together.

Rhett and Tessa decided to leave as soon as they were done eating, their craving for alone time with each other made evident by their public displays of affection. I was ready to go when they were, but for some reason, Adeline stalled and suggested we have one more drink. She seemed nervous to be alone with me, so I indulged her by going to the bar to order our drinks since we'd already paid our dinner bill. I place our drink order and pay the bartender once they are ready. With drinks in hand, I maneuver myself out of the crowd and stop dead in my tracks when I see a strange man sitting with Adeline at our table. I watch him place his hand on her thigh and anger starts to rage inside of me.

"Take your hand off my thigh before you lose a testicle courtesy of my heel," I hear her tell him and if I wasn't feeling so violent right about now, I would've laughed and enjoyed seeing the appearance of Adeline the Firecracker. But seeing this asshole's hand on her makes me see red.

"You heard her, take your hands off her," I growl as I approach the table, slapping down the drinks so hard that beer spills out of them, splashing onto his pants.

He looks me up and down with a menacing look. "And who in the hell are you to tell me what to do?"

"I'm her boyfriend, that's who." I take a step forward, the tips of my boots touching his own shoes. I mentally count to ten, hoping this guy leaves peacefully.

"Chill out, man. I didn't realize she was with someone," he sneers while standing up and getting into my personal space. My hands fist at my sides, ready to pound him into oblivion, but Rhett's words of no trouble resonate through me.

"I think you're the one who needs to chill out." Before I realize what's about to happen, Adeline grabs one of the beers and pours it over his head. He screams and closes his eyes from the sting of the beer and that's when I use the opportunity to punch him in his nose. He goes down hard, but I don't look back as I grab Adeline's hand and we race for the door. We don't stop running until we get to her car and throw ourselves in it. She turns on the engine, reverses the car with a jerk and races out of the parking lot. Fortunately, the hotel is only two blocks away from the restaurant.

"I can't believe that just happened," she exclaims in excitement, her chest rising and falling from trying to catch her breath.

"I can't believe you poured a beer over his head!" I laugh, my heart bursting with pride over her actions. I know I shouldn't be promoting violence, but I'm damn proud of her for sticking up for herself. "That was sexy as hell, Adi."

She pulls into the hotel parking lot and jerks us to a stop in one of their open spots. She parks the car, turns off the engine and looks at me. "I've never had a man stick up for me the way you did tonight." Her voice is husky, her eyes filled with desire as she stares at me with carnal need.

Seconds tick by, the air in the car filled with electric, sexual tension. All of sudden, we're both reaching for each other at the same time, our lips fusing into one, tongues thrashing against each other.

"I need you, Adeline. I need you now," I moan as she kisses along my jawline before latching onto my earlobe, sending shivers down my spine.

"Let's go inside," I plead, my growing erection becoming unbearable. She nods and we untangle ourselves hastily to get out of the car. We walk briskly to our room in silence, no words needed as the anticipation of what's to come grows inside us.

I unlock my room with my card key, grab her hand and pull her inside. Once the door shuts, the room is encased in darkness, but I know exactly where she is by her delicious scent. I grab her by her neck and reclaim her lips, teasing them with my tongue until she opens for me. We moan at the same time, our hands immediately grabbing at each other's clothing and pulling each item off. My shirt and her dress hit the floor while she guides me toward the bed and pushes me down. My breath hitches in my throat as my eyes drink in her beauty, my tongue ready to lick every single curve of that soft body. Her eyes are hooded with passion, telling me she wants me just as badly as I want her. She bites her bottom lip and reaches for my pants, unbuttons them, and slowly pulls down my zipper. She snakes her fingers inside my boxers to wrap around my erection. I gasp at her touch and sigh loudly when her fingers encircle me and squeeze. While she starts pumping me, my fingers skim over her satin panties, my thumb connecting with her clit over the soaked fabric. She moans and arches her back as I press harder over her sensitive area.

"I want this, Ryan," she tells me, her voice raspy from pleasure. She captures my mouth with hers and lowers herself to straddle me. My hands work their way up her back to the clasp of her bra. My skilled fingers quickly unhook it and I push the straps down her arms. As soon as her breasts are free, my mouth latches on to one of her swollen nipples. She purrs loudly, clasping my head as close to her chest as she can. While I suck harder, her hips start to gyrate against me, her hands working up and down my shaft that's standing straight against her stomach. I pay attention to her other breast, but my concentration soon wavers when I feel her rub my pre-cum over my sensitive tip.

I grasp her hips and gently nudge her to my side to lay down. Once she's on her back, I grab hold of the waistband of her panties and bring them down her hips and legs. I stand up and remove the condom that I placed in my pocket earlier, hoping that this night would go exactly as its going. She watches me slide my jeans down my legs and step out of them. She licks her lips when I free my cock from my boxers, almost making me explode at the sight of her. I remove the condom from its packaging and roll it down over me. I lean down and slowly start kissing my way up her calf, over her knee and along her thigh until I get to that sweet spot between her legs.

I ease her thighs open and drag my finger along her slit until I flick over her bud. I start playing with it, first with my fingers and then with my tongue. Her whimpers get louder with each lick, her noises driving me to the brink of no return. Her hands rake through my hair, gripping my head while she rocks against my mouth. She moves faster, pulling me against her harder and I know she's close to coming.

"Get in me now, Ryan," she softly demands and I can't help but chuckle at her bossiness.

"Your wish is my command, little minx." I crawl over her and drop my forehead to hers as I sink inside her satiny heat, both of us moaning at how amazing it feels. Once her walls start to clench around me in adjustment, I slowly start rocking my hips.

"You feel like heaven," I whisper while gently thrusting into her. My lips find hers and soon our tongues are mimicking our hips. She wraps her legs tightly around my waist and starts matching my thrusts. Our bodies start to move faster, harder, and I break our kiss so I can watch her climax. Her eyes meet mine while she grabs my ass and squeezes hard. Her walls are pulsating around me, clenching to the point that's about to make me come. I pull my torso up and balance myself on my forearms, arching my back slightly so that my pelvis grinds harder against her. It only takes a few more deep thrusts when I feel her walls squeeze tightly around me as she screams out her orgasm, igniting my own intense release.

I'm floating down from the most incredible high I've ever experienced being inside of a woman. I don't think this feeling is so powerful because of abstinence. This feels different.

Adeline is different.

As the night passes into early morning dawn, we continue our sexual explorations of each other. Our last bout of sex seems frantic for her, as if she's kissing me for the very last time. After we've climaxed again and she falls asleep while cuddling, I wonder why she seemed to be more emotional this time. I refuse to believe that this will be our final time together.

If anything, it's only the beginning.

# Chapter 12

## Adeline

I MADE SURE I had zero expectation of hearing from Ryan during his four-week absence, yet every day he surprised me with a text message in the morning and followed up with a phone call at night. I told myself each day that this might be the day you don't hear from him anymore and to cherish my memories with him. Since my heart was so delicate with our unknown future, I purposely didn't follow his performances for fear I would see photos of him with other women, annihilating my heart to ashes.

Tessa released another book during their absence that hit *USA Today Bestseller's List*, prompting her to finally turn in her resignation at the rodeo. This will truly be the last rodeo she works, so our plans to move to Austin will happen quicker than we expected. This led me to rip the Band-Aid off and have a conversation with my father about transferring dealerships. At first, he wasn't happy and refused my request. When I explained to him that I needed my own identity and not be known just as Clint Murphy's daughter, he finally seemed to understand my desire to move to a bigger city where I'm anonymous.

Reluctantly, he agreed to do it whenever I was ready.

But Tessa and I didn't seem to be in any hurry, both of us hesitant to make a big move until we knew what was happening with our green-eyed cowboys. Especially since they go back to Ireland during their break, which I learned about from Tessa and not Ryan.

I was hurt when she told me, wondering why he wasn't the one telling me this information. When a week went by and he still didn't mention anything, I started to believe that his silence was because that was the excuse he was going to use to end things.

That night I sent him a text saying I didn't feel good and would talk with him the next day.

It was mostly the truth since I was sick from a broken heart.

"You're being ridiculous," Tessa chided when she discovered me in bed, crying. "Just because he hasn't said anything doesn't mean he's breaking up with you!"

"There is no relationship to break since he doesn't consider us exclusive," I whined, a fresh wave of tears spilling down my cheeks.

"Didn't you say he told the asshole in the bar that you're his girlfriend?"

"He was only doing that to get the guy away from me," I sniffed, not wanting to remember how incredible that night turned out to be.

"Regardless, he's called you every night since being away. Of course he thinks you're dating. He's just hasn't mastered communicating while being in a relationship." That did sound like Ryan since he's never been in a serious relationship before.

"He's probably just spending time with me because he's bored and why not have a warm body since Rhett is with you?" I pouted, my theory sounding more logical the more I thought about it.

"Oh you've got it bad for him because that's the most asinine thing you've ever said!"

I rolled my eyes at her, wishing she'd just let me wallow in my own self-pity for once.

"Maybe he hasn't mentioned Ireland yet because he's scared that *you* will dump *him*. Ever think of that, Adi? You're a catch. He should be worried about losing you. Guys are more sensitive than you think."

That didn't sound like Ryan at all.

My emotional state put me in a deep sleep and I woke up the following morning with a fresh mind. I continued talking with him, not letting him know I knew about Ireland and acted as if nothing was wrong between us.

I immersed myself into work at the dealership and work for myself with my graphic design business. I continued attending my brother's football games. Keeping myself busy made the weeks fly by and before I knew it, Ryan was back in town. He asked me to stay with him in his hotel while Rhett moved into our apartment to be with Tessa. I was a ball of nerves driving to the hotel, but we attacked each other as soon as he opened the hotel room door. I called in sick the next day and we spent twenty-four hours straight in bed. Living with him in the hotel for that week was like a dream, with the best naughty hotel sex I'd ever experienced. It felt like we were on our honeymoon and I never wanted it to end. He asked me to go to Mexico with him the following week after the rodeo and my heart burst with excitement, ignoring the warnings that my brain was screaming at me about how he still has not said a word about Ireland.

SATURDAY HAD ARRIVED and I'm a nervous wreck. Not because I have to watch Ryan being jerked around by a ginormous bull again, but because we only have one more week together before he leaves for Ireland and he still has been radio silent on the subject.

*Maybe he's taking you to Mexico because he feels guilty?*

*Maybe he's taking you to Mexico to break-up with you?*

*Maybe you've become psycho and he should break up with you!*

If things don't work out with Ryan, I'm done with love and will be celibate for the rest of my life.

I take forever to get ready, dreading going to this rodeo when I should be celebrating with Tessa that this is her last day of work. I'm also dreading seeing my family, who will be in attendance. They know I've been living in sin with Ryan all week long, my father giving me disapproving looks whenever he sees me, while my mother is waiting to plan the non-existent wedding.

The vibration of my phone snaps me out of my thoughts and I see a text message from Ryan flashing on its screen.

**Ryan: I can't wait to see your beautiful face in the stands today. Dinner with your family after?**

**Me: Hell no! Straight to the hotel for congratulatory sex on your huge victory.**

**Ryan: My kind of woman!**

*Am I really though?* I wanted to ask him.

*Ugh, get out of your head, Adeline, and just enjoy your time with him.*

I finish my make-up and take a deep breath to calm my nerves. Satisfied with how I look, I grab my purse and car keys and drive to the rodeo.

I text Tessa and Ryan when I arrive and sit with my family. I scan the crowd to see if I can find Tessa, who usually works during the whole time. *I wonder if she'll let me hide out in her office.*

"Ryan's stats are impressive," my older brother, Colt, remarks while reading the program on the cowboys.

"Since when do you know about bull riding statistics?" I look at him skeptically because football is the only game he ever pays attention too.

"Since my sister started dating a bull rider." He gives me a knowing look, the corners of his mouth tipping up into a grin. I throw my arm around his shoulders and give him a side hug. Even though I'm the eldest sibling, Colt always has been protective over me.

The saddle bronc competition is coming up next and I text Tessa so she can sit with us to watch Rhett. We don't clap when Tessa's ex-boyfriend competes, but we make sure we are loud and cheer for Rhett. He performs perfectly, making Tessa emotional with joy.

"I'm going to go downstairs and congratulate Rhett. I'll be back!" She takes off running to see him.

The bull riding competition is next and although I don't think he has his phone on him, I send Ryan a good luck text. I close my eyes during the first two performances, my stomach becoming queasy when I hear the crowd gasp in horror when one of the riders falls off the bull.

*Please, God, keep Ryan safe!* I chant in my head over and over again.

"Are you going to keep your eyes closed like that and continue rocking back and forth, chanting? Because you look like you're possessed by the devil himself," Carson states, staring at me as if I'm crazy.

"I don't think I can watch this," I mumble when I see Ryan walking toward the chute where the bull is waiting for him. If I wasn't so nervous, I would take the time to appreciate how hot he looks in his chaps.

"Adeline, when do you leave for Mexico again?" my mother asks, distracting me from my fantasy of naked Ryan only wearing his chaps to bed.

"Monday morning," I respond, my eyes focused on him as he mounts the bull.

"Oh good, then we have time to go shopping for Ireland tomorrow."

"We what?" I whip my head around to look at her. Clearly, she made a mistake and meant Mexico instead of Ireland.

"Ireland, darling. You need appropriate clothes for Ireland. It's very cold there this time of year."

"Mother, don't you mean Mexico where it's warm and sunny all year round?"

"No, Adeline. Ryan called your father and asked him for permission to take you to Ireland. He never called and asked if he could take you to Mexico, which completely ruffled your daddy's feathers by the way." She whispers the last part so that my father doesn't hear her, but I completely ignore what she's saying as her words sink into my brain. No wonder Ryan hasn't said anything since this was probably going to be a surprise that my mother just ruined.

I have been misjudging him this whole time.

*If he's taking me to Mexico and Ireland, does this mean he might actually love me?*

I have zero time to react as the buzzer sounds and Ryan's body settles into a synchronized rhythm with the bucking of the bull. My eyes are wide open, mesmerized at his athleticism. I scream in excitement as soon as the eight-seconds are over with, cheering as loud as I can so Ryan can hear me.

His ride was perfection.

*He's* perfection.

He finds me in the crowd and blows a kiss before waving at everyone and heading back to the dressing room.

"I'll be back," I tell my family and before they can even respond, I'm running downstairs.

There's a huge crowd surrounding him when I get backstage. I make my way through the bodies and as soon as our eyes lock, I hurl myself at him. He hoists me up and I automatically wrap my legs around his waist. I crash my mouth into his, needing to show him through my kisses how proud I am of him. I can hear the lightbulbs flashing, but I don't care if we make the news. Let the whole world know that he's mine.

"You were magnificent," I whisper into his ear as he trickles kisses down my neck.

"Only because you're here. You're like my muse, my good luck charm. You make me want to be the best in front you. I focus more knowing my little minx is in the crowd watching me, hopefully getting very turned on as she sees me ride that big, nasty bull," he teases in my ear, causing me to laugh at his wickedness.

"You always turn me on," I sigh, wishing we were already back in the hotel so I could show him how much he lights my whole body on fire.

"You think for forever?" I look at him in surprise, my eyebrows arching at the word "forever."

"I'm a better man with you by my side, Adi, and I want that to be forever." He puts me down as he sees tears pooling in my eyes.

"Tell me you'll be mine, forever, Adeline. Tell me you love me," he commands and all I can do is nod, incapable of speaking because the words I've been waiting to hear from him echo throughout my brain and settle into my heart.

"I love you, Ryan Kearney," I barely croak out before he claims my lips with a heart-melting kiss.

"I love you more, my little minx."

THE END ... FOR NOW!

# Bear Creek Rodeo Series

The Bear Creek Rodeo Series are insta-love short stories written by Jennifer D. Bokal, Amy L. Gale, Sara Jolene, Jessica Marin and Kirsten Osbourne. All stories in the series are stand-alone novellas and can be read in no particular order.

Add all Bear Creek Rodeo books to your GOODREADS

Follow all the authors on Social Media

Amy L. Gale

Jessica Marin

Sara Jolene

Jennifer D. Bokal

Kirsten Osbourne

# Also by Jessica Marin

### The Let Me In Series

Heartbreak Warfare (Let Me In, Book 1)

Perfectly Lonely (Let Me In, Book 2)

Edge of Desire (Let Me In, Book 3)

Half of My Heart (Let Me In, Book 4 - Cal's POV)

### Standalone Novels

Until Valerie: Happily Ever Alpha World

Love At The Bluebird

(co-written with Aurora Rose Reynolds)

Shopping For Love

### Bear Creek Rodeo

The Irish Cowboy

The Celtic Cowboy

# Acknowledgments

It was a huge honor to be asked by Sara Jolene to be part of this incredible series. I hadn't read many contemporary western romances featuring cowboys and rodeos before, so I was excited for the challenge and was able to discover new authors in my research. I hope you enjoyed Rhett and Tessa's story!

Thank you to all of the readers and bloggers who take the time out of your day to read my work and support me. Your positive feedback and love mean the world to me.

Thank you to my family, especially my husband and children. Without their support, I wouldn't be able to continue living my dream.

It truly takes a village to make a book come alive and I couldn't have done it without the following people: Andrea Cloyd, Brittany Holland, Emma Mack, Shelly Utley and Tracey Vuolo.

Thank you to my Misfits for your continued love, support and promotion of all things Jessica Marin.

Please make sure you follow me on all of my social media pages and sign up for my newsletter at authorjessicamarin.com to be up to date with upcoming releases and book signings.

I look forward to our next adventure together!

Peace and love,

Jessica

# About the Author

Jessica Marin began her love affair with books at a young age from the encouragement of her Grandma Shirley. She has always dreamed of being an author and finally made her dreams of writing happily ever after stories a reality. She currently resides in Tennessee with her husband, children and fur babies. When she's not hanging out with her family, she loves watching a good movie, going dancing with the ladies, sniffing essential oils, daydreaming of warm beaches, and world peace.

Jessica would love for you to connect with her on Facebook, Instagram, TikTok and Pinterest.